# AVON'S VELVET GLOVE SERIES

"THE VELVET GLOVE SERIES WILL BECOME AN EXCITING ALTERNATIVE TO THE STRAIGHT ROMANCE. ALL OF THE SENSUALITY AND MAGNETISM OF ROMANCES IS THERE AND ALSO THE 'CLIFF-HANGING' TENSENESS OF GOOD SUSPENSE."

*Affaire de Coeur*

"IT'S WHAT WE FEEL IS A NEW TREND IN ROMANTIC FICTION—ROMANTIC SUSPENSE."

Kathryn Falk,
*Romantic Times*

"THE VELVET GLOVE LINE IS GEARED TO ROMANTIC SUSPENSE . . .THE SURVIVAL OF LOVE HOLDS THE READER IN AS MUCH SUSPENSE AS THE DANGER."

Terri Busch,
*Heart Line*

Avon Books publishes a new Velvet Glove book each month. Ask for them at your bookstore.

*Other Books in the*
**Velvet Glove Series:**

LOVE'S SUSPECT *by Betty Henrichs*
DANGEROUS ENCHANTMENT *by Jean Hager*
THE WILDFIRE TRACE *by Cathy Gillen Thacker*
IN THE DEAD OF THE NIGHT *by Rachel Scott*
THE KNOTTED SKEIN *by Carla Neggers*
LIKE A LOVER *by Lynn Michaels*
THE HUNTED HEART *by Barbara Doyle*
FORBIDDEN DREAMS *by Jolene Prewit-Parker*
TENDER BETRAYAL *by Virginia Smiley*
FIRES AT MIDNIGHT *by Marie Flasschoen*
STRANGERS IN EDEN *by Peggy Mercer*
THE UNEVEN SCORE *by Carla Neggers*
TAINTED GOLD *by Lynn Michaels*
A TOUCH OF SCANDAL *by Leslie Davis*
AN UNCERTAIN CHIME *by Lizabeth Loghry*
MASKED REFLECTIONS *by Dee Stuart*
THE SPLINTERED MOON *by Leslie Davis*

*Look for Upcoming Titles in the*
**Velvet Glove Series:**

STALK A STRANGER *by Rachel Scott*
JAMAICAN MIDNIGHT *by Sherryl Woods*
THE TANGLED MESH *by Lee Karr*
DAUGHTER OF JOY *by Marianne Joyce*

Velvet Glove

20

# Lynn Michaels

# A Lover's Gift

AVON
PUBLISHERS OF BARD, CAMELOT, DISCUS AND FLARE BOOKS

A LOVER'S GIFT is an original publication of Avon Books. This work has never before appeared in book form. This work is a novel. Any similarity to actual persons or events is purely coincidental.

AVON BOOKS
A division of
The Hearst Corporation
1790 Broadway
New York, New York 10019


Published by arrangement with Velvet Glove, Inc.
Library of Congress Catalog Card Number: 85-91840
ISBN: 0-380-89786-5



First Avon Printing, August 1985



Printed in the U. S. A.

WFH 10 9 8 7 6 5 4 3 2 1

For Glo

# A LOVER'S GIFT

# Chapter One

USUALLY, because she gained five pounds if she so much as sniffed a margarita, Aubrey steered clear of alcoholic beverages. For the same reason she avoided desserts and sauces, but Sara blithely ignored her murmured objections and ordered coq au vin, broccoli with hollandaise sauce, a bottle of white wine, and chocolate mousse.

"You have just doomed me," Aubrey told her unhappily as she handed her menu to the waiter and he bowed away from their table. "You, my dear friend, have condemned me to a two-day fast and ten extra sit-ups for the next week."

"We are celebrating," Sara replied airily. "This is your first night in New York and *my* birthday—ergo, I refuse to eat like a gerbil."

Sara was the only person Aubrey had ever met who actually used the word *ergo* in conversation. She'd fallen in love with that archaic little adverb in a course titled "Shakespeare for the Theater" during their sophomore year at Stephens College. For weeks it had been *ergo this* and *ergo that* every time she'd opened her mouth—until Aubrey had been ready to scream. Now she smiled.

"Okay, Draper." She narrowed one eye and

pointed an index finger at her. "Tonight we indulge, but tomorrow you hit the exercise mat with me."

"Ugh." Sara wrinkled her small, perfect nose and tilted her head to one side. "Why don't I cancel the wine instead?"

"Cancel the mousse."

"But it's my favorite!"

"It goes straight to the hips."

"Not *my* hips," she retorted.

"At your age, Sara, not to mention your profession," Aubrey replied earnestly, folding her hands on the table edge and leaning forward, "you really should start watching what you eat."

"My *age!*" she shot back indignantly. "Look here, Nichols, you're only four months shy of the big three-oh yourself."

"True," Aubrey agreed, a tiny smile tugging at the corners of her mouth, "but then I eat like a gerbil—which is the reason I no longer look like one."

She crossed her eyes and puffed out her cheeks, and Sara laughed. Several heads, most of them male, Aubrey noted, turned admiring glances in her direction.

That image—of Sara, her lovely face flushed and animated, her blue eyes glistening with pinpoints of light—remained crystalline and vivid in Aubrey's recollections of that night. So did the mousse—which they argued over so long that it arrived at the table before they'd settled the issue—in capital letters as The Last Dessert Before the Storm.

"Oh, God, I'm in agony," Sara groaned once they'd finished their meal, paid their check, and walked through the dark-paneled, dimly lit restaurant toward the exit. "Which one of the seven deadly sins is gluttony?" She rubbed one hand on her midriff beneath the paisley shawl draped over her white cossack blouse and shoved open the heavy, carved door with the other.

"I'm not sure," Aubrey replied vaguely, blinking to clear the warm rush of the wine that fuzzed her brain and her travel-wearied eyes as she pushed through the door behind Sara. "But in my book"—she faltered and sucked a shallow breath as the humid summer night engulfed her—"it's always been numero uno."

The sticky blackness and hot, exhaust-tainted breeze rocked her slightly on her heels. Her vision blurred, the garish neon tubes lighting the front of the restaurant bled and swam together, and for an awful moment as her throat constricted and the ever-present traffic noises on Columbus Avenue roared in her ears, she thought she was going to be sick on the sidewalk.

"Steady, girl." Sara caught her elbow and laughed gently. "You should have let me cancel the wine."

"I wish I had." She smiled weakly and brushed away the heavy strands of auburn hair blown across her face by the sluggish, muggy breeze.

"Never fear, Grandma Draper's Remedy is close at hand. C'mon, let's save cab fare and walk home—Eighty-seventh Street isn't far."

Firmly wrapping Aubrey's fingers around the curve of her right elbow, Sara wheeled on her left heel. She managed half a step before Aubrey balked and jerked Sara around to face her.

"What do you mean *walk?*" she demanded. "It's dark and this is New York City."

"Oh, for God's sake, Bree, don't be such a *hick.*" Sara made a face and yanked her down the sidewalk. "This is real life, not an episode of 'Cagney and Lacey.' "

Pulled off balance by the sharp tug on her arm, Aubrey stumbled along behind her, dodging and ducking her way around other pedestrians. By the time Aubrey had her feet firmly beneath her again, Sara had towed her across a street and had covered another half a block. So far so good, she thought, but wished the canister of Mace her mother had given her was in her skirt pocket—where Adelia Nichols had told her to keep it—rather than in her purse. It wouldn't do her any good in her handbag, her mother had cautioned—so naturally, that's where Aubrey had put it.

"See, oh timid one?" Sara taunted with a smile as she released her death grip on Aubrey's hand and untied the knotted ends of her shawl. "We've walked almost two blocks and we haven't been accosted by a mugger or a rapist yet."

"How much farther is your building?"

"Four blocks."

"Then I'd say gloating is a bit premature," Aubrey answered and unzipped her oversized briefcase bag as she tugged it off her shoulder.

"Save your Mace," Sara told her. "Mine's in my pocket."

"I thought you said this was real life," Aubrey reminded her as she zipped her bag and sidestepped a couple walking hand-in-hand toward them, "and not an episode of 'Cagney and Lacey.' "

"You really *are* a hick, aren't you?" Sara

glanced her a frown and raised one eyebrow. "Is this the reason it's taken me almost six years to browbeat you into coming to New York? You're *afraid?"*

"I'm not afraid, Sara," Aubrey denied firmly. "Nervous, yes, and the only reason I'm here is to research my doctoral thesis at NYU. I explained all that in my letter."

"Yes, you did," Sara agreed as she caught and held the fringed ends of her shawl in her hands. "But as I recall, you were very vague and nebulous about the details of your trip until I wrote back and told you that Jack would probably fly in from San Diego for the Fourth."

Uh-oh, here we go again, Aubrey thought, just as the toe of her right sandal bumped a crack in the sidewalk. She tripped forward three steps into a pool of pale light beneath a street lamp, pulled herself upright, and glanced over her shoulder at Sara.

"Gotcha." Sara grinned and jerked her shawl free of her shoulders with a snapping, Zorro-like flourish.

"Got me what?" Aubrey asked blankly as she stood flat-footed in the middle of the walk and waited for Sara to catch up.

"Obtusity ill becomes you, Bree." She stopped beside her and tickled one end of the shawl in her face.

"The word is *obtuseness,"* Aubrey corrected her as she batted the fringe out of her eyes.

"Thank you, Madame English Teacher." Sara smirked and tossed her shawl over her left arm. "You know, I find it extremely interesting that my big brother was also very iffy about the Fourth until I told him *you* would be here." She smiled slyly and wagged her eyebrows again.

"So what?" Aubrey asked flatly, hoping she sounded convincingly bewildered.

"So I think we'll finish this conversation once I've administered Grandma Draper's Remedy." Sara caught her arm again and propelled her toward the corner. "We're getting nowhere fast."

"What exactly is this magic cure-all?"

"Hair of the dog, my dear," Sara replied, a determined edge in her voice as she tightened her grip on Aubrey's arm and increased their pace.

Smiling, Aubrey let Sara march her briskly down the sidewalk. This had to be at least the fifteen thousandth time that she'd managed to avoid her friend's not-so-subtle efforts to trap her into admitting that she'd been in love with Jack since she and Sara had been freshmen at Stephens. Her latest tactic—get her drunk and she'll bare her soul—smacked of desperation; still, it amused Aubrey and made her wonder why Sara hadn't thought of it long ago.

As bright as she was, and as close a friendship as they'd managed to maintain despite the miles separating New York and Springfield, Illinois, it never ceased to amaze Aubrey that Sara hadn't long ago found a way to wring a confession out of her. Maybe it was her face, still disgustingly round (although her slightly dimpled chin at least *showed* now that she no longer had cheeks like a chipmunk), or her milk-chocolate brown eyes that gave her such a wide-eyed, sincere look. Or maybe, she concluded with a wry smile—as Sara hauled her around the corner onto her block filled with pleasant brownstones and small apartment buildings—just maybe she'd missed her true calling. Maybe she should've majored in drama instead and gone on the stage with Sara.

About a third of the way down the well-lit street, other sounds—the steady thrum of air conditioners, the barking of a dog—overrode the roar of the traffic on the busier avenue behind them, which had faded now to a throaty, muted whine. Though the leaves on the few small trees planted along the sidewalk barely stirred in the nearly fetid breeze, Aubrey felt cooler walking beneath their heat-wilted branches.

"Does anyone ever water them?" she asked, and frowned sympathetically at a thin, bedraggled specimen that in the darkness looked like it could be either an ornamental maple or an ash.

"Water what?" Sara returned, easing her grip on Aubrey's arm as they turned up the steps to her building.

"The trees," she answered, still gazing at the scrawny little thing over her shoulder.

"I haven't the faintest idea," Sara replied in a voice that said she couldn't care less.

I'll give that one a drink tomorrow, Aubrey decided, then turned her head to watch where she was going as she stumbled up a step. The lobby lights glaring through the glass front of the building burned her tired eyes and made them water. She blinked rapidly and smiled at Sam, the stocky, sixtyish doorman, who pushed open the heavy glass portal from the inside.

"Evening, Miss Draper, Miss Nichols." He nodded and touched the bill of the gray cap pushed back on his thinning salt and pepper hair. "Did you enjoy your dinner?"

"I overjoyed, as usual," Sara told him, grimacing as she tugged Aubrey through the door behind her.

He grinned and chuckled. Still blinking to clear her misted eyes, Aubrey cast him a backward smile as Sara towed her across the red and white tiled lobby. He winked at her, she winked back—though it only worsened the film over her eyes—and decided that she was going to like Sam very much.

"Why are you crying?" Sara asked, smiling mischievously as she drew her to a halt before the elevator and pushed the button. "All choked up at the thought of seeing Jack again?"

"Hardly." Aubrey made a face and wiped her mascara-thickened lashes on her index fingers. "I've got something in my eyes, I think."

"Stars, I'm sure," Sara returned with a grin.

"Pollution, *I'm* sure," Aubrey corrected her and lowered her black-smeared fingers.

Her vision was still blurred, but pleasantly, and she smiled at the prisms of light she saw around the lamps illuminating the lobby.

"This is better than rose-colored glasses," she told Sara. "All the lights have little rainbows around them."

"Pollution, indeed!" Sara laughed, took her elbow again as the elevator opened, and led her into the car. "You've got a buzz on."

"I do *not,*" she denied vehemently, and shivered as a draft of cold air from the ceiling duct seeped down the perspiration-dampened back of her neck.

"Sober people don't see rainbows, Bree," Sara informed her with a grin, and led her out of the elevator as the doors opened on the third floor.

Though the plush, dark red carpeting in the corridor muffled their footsteps, the floorboards underneath groaned as they walked toward Sara's door. The hallway smelled pleasantly of old wood, and Aubrey, tiring rapidly of the rainbows, wished her eyes would clear so she could make out the pattern in the ivory wallpaper.

"I think I'll wash off my mascara," she said, groping her way into the living room once Sara had unlocked the paneled walnut door and shoved it open.

"It won't help!"

In the bedroom doorway, Aubrey half-turned and stuck out her tongue at Sara's blurry shape near the bar that separated the minuscule kitchen from the living room. She laughed, and Aubrey bumped her way around the doorjamb into the bathroom.

She rinsed a washcloth in the sink, pressed it to her eyes, and sighed. The wet terry-cloth square only gummed her mascara, but the cool water felt so *good.* Hollering at Sara that she was going to take a shower, she stripped off her clothes and stepped into the tub. Afterward, wrapped in a thick blue towel, Aubrey attacked her gluey lashes with cleansing cream.

That's the last time I'll use waterproof mascara, she vowed, still blinking at the misty residue clouding her vision. Shivering a little, she slipped into her pajamas and walked barefoot through the bedroom into the living room.

On a pile of pastel floor cushions thrown on the gray shag carpet, Sara was sitting in a lavender nightie. The nineteen-inch color portable mounted on a cherry wall unit was tuned to the late news, and Sara's eyes were fixed on the screen while she clamped a corkscrew over the top of a dark green wine bottle.

Behind her on a low modern sidetable squatted a fat, pink ceramic lamp with a pleated white shade; next to it in a wooden frame sat a picture of Jack. Abruptly, as Aubrey blinked at his dark auburn hair shining in the glow of the lamp and his smiling green eyes, the mist cleared and the rainbows vanished.

"Hurry up with that, will you?" she asked. "I think my buzz is wearing off."

Sara glanced up at her, started to laugh, and toppled over onto the cushions. In the hollow of her throat gleamed the heart-shaped gold locket Jack had sent her from San Diego for her birthday. A tiny diamond chip mounted in its scrolled center winked at Aubrey as she crossed the room and dropped onto a lime green cushion opposite Sara.

"Why in hell," she chuckled, pushing herself up on her hands, "are you still wearing your fat-jams?"

"You remembered!" Aubrey grinned and plucked at the front of her nearly threadbare, blue striped size-sixteen pajamas. "I wear them to remind me what life was like when I was a two-legged dumpling."

"Bree." Sara looked at her steadily as she picked up the wine bottle. "Jack calls you Dumpling for the same reason he calls me Sara Heartburn. It's a term of affection."

"I know that, Sara." Aubrey smiled as she leaned toward the coffee table and retrieved the two crystal goblets that sat there. "Still, it was a whale of a motivation to lose forty-five pounds."

"Well, I certainly hope you brought along a negligee." Sara grunted and crooked her tongue in one corner of her mouth as she twisted the corkscrew.

"I don't own a negligee," Aubrey told her. "I'm not the negligee type."

"You don't have to be the type, Bree," Sara replied between clenched teeth as the screw bit through the cork and she struggled to pull it out again. "You just have to wear one when we go to the farm for the Fourth. Mother and Dad'll be back from their cruise by then, did I tell you?"

"No, you didn't, and why do I have to wear a negligee?"

The cork came free with a loud pop and Sara set it aside on the carpet. She braced her hands on her folded knees and wrinkled her nose. "Who do you think you're going to seduce in your fat-jams?"

"I know who I'd like to seduce."

"Oh, yeah?" Sara grinned, wiggled forward on her tailbone, and filled the wineglasses. "Who, as if I didn't know?"

Aubrey's gaze slid to the left where the "Nightline" logo had just appeared on the television screen. "Ted Koppel," she sighed dreamily.

*"What?"* Sara shrieked.

"If you don't mind"—Aubrey frowned at Sara's thunderstruck expression over her shoulder as she shifted her position on the cushion—"this is my favorite show and I'm trying to watch—" In midsentence her breath caught in her throat and a fearful chill crawled up her back as Ted Koppel's well-modulated voice caught and held her attention.

". . . although FBI spokesmen are still declining comment at this hour, John Collins, president of Nu-Lite Laboratories, did confirm that correspondence between Dr. Jack Draper and a representative of a foreign government—correspondence alluding heavily to the LC-15 project which Dr. Draper has been developing for Nu-Lite—had been found this afternoon in his San Diego apartment. When asked if the letters, exchanged over a period of eight months, concerned Dr. Draper's alleged intent to sell LC-15 to this as yet unidentified foreign power, Mr. Collins refused to comment further. . . ."

Involuntarily, the breath trapped in Aubrey's throat expelled itself and she sucked a startled half-gasp of air as she whirled on her knees to face a pale and stricken Sara. Her blue eyes, wide and slowly filling with tears, were riveted to the TV screen. Swallowing the lump that had suddenly risen to her throat, Aubrey took the wine bottle out of her hands, put it down on the coffee table, and wrapped the fingers of her right hand around Sara's wrist. Pressing her left hand to her own rapidly yammering heart, she looked back at Ted Koppel. Behind his left shoulder, Jack's picture—the same one sitting on the table beside the mauve and cream striped sofa—smiled at her.

"One of the country's leading researchers in the field of laser physics, Dr. Draper was last seen this afternoon with Hugh Lawrence, owner of Lawrence Laboratories in San Diego. When approached by reporters outside FBI headquarters earlier this evening, Mr. Lawrence declined to comment on the LC-15 project or the whereabouts of Dr. Draper, who is still wanted for questioning by FBI officials in San Diego."

Beneath her own none-too-steady fingers, Aubrey felt gooseflesh rise on Sara's thin, cold wrist. The station went to a commercial, and she picked up the remote control from the corner of the coffee table. It felt like a lump of lead in her clammy palm, and her thumb trembled on the button as she switched off the set. She scooted around on her knees to face Sara, glanced up as she did, and felt a wrench between her ribs as her gaze fell and locked on Jack's photograph.

"Oh, Ted, how *could* you," she whispered, and blinked back tears that pricked hotly behind her eyes.

"It's a lie, Bree," Sara said thickly. "It's all a lie."

"Of course it is," Aubrey replied woodenly, even though she knew that it wasn't.

As desperately as she wanted to believe that the report wasn't true, she knew that network news programs didn't air fabricated or unsubstantiated stories. Oh, Jack, she wanted to scream at his picture, *why?*

"You believe it, don't you?"

The bitter edge in Sara's voice startled Aubrey and pulled her gaze away from the photograph. With a half-guilty jerk of her hand on Sara's wrist, she glanced at her over her shoulder.

"How could you believe that garbage?" Sara shrilled at her as she twisted her hand free of Aubrey's and wiped the tears spilling down her cheeks. "You love him, for God's sake, how can you believe that crap?"

"Sara . . ." Aubrey pleaded, reaching to take her hand again.

"Leave me alone!" she cried and wrenched herself to her feet.

Arms folded and shoulders hunched, Sara withdrew to the tiny window seat near the small, round dining table. Rising on her knees to look over the back of the hide-a-bed, Aubrey watched Sara huddle there in a miserable knot, the fingers of her right hand tangling in the chain of the locket as she stared out the window at the street below, sobbing.

# Chapter Two

WHY, Aubrey wondered with a sharp stab of guilt, why couldn't she have lied—just *once?* Sinking down on her heels again, she leaned her left elbow against the sofa cushion and curled her fingers against her temple. Her own eyes swam as she listened to Sara, but she swiped furiously at her tears and managed to ask in a reasonably level voice, "Do you want me to go home?"

Sara stopped sobbing and drew a shaky, tremulous breath. "Oh, God, *please* don't, Bree. I-I just can't face this alone," she stammered, and started to cry again.

No great, wracking sobs now, just a quiet, heartbroken whimper. Refusing to look at Jack's photograph, Aubrey pushed herself to her feet and walked to the gray Formica bar which separated the kitchen from the living room. She picked up the box of pink Posh Puffs tissues that sat there and carried it to the window seat. With tear-soaked, mascara-blackened eyes, Sara looked up at her and smiled weakly.

"Th-thanks," she sniffed as she took the box. She plucked several tissues, blew her nose, then drew up her legs and folded them beneath her, giving Aubrey enough room to wiggle onto the seat, face her, and do the same. "I'm sorry, Bree," she apologized shakily. "I didn't mean what I said."

"Forget it." Aubrey smiled. "I have already."

"Damn Jack anyway!" Sara cried angrily and hurled her wadded fistful of Puffs at his picture. She missed, of course, and the ball of pink tissues rolled under the table. "He'd better hope the FBI finds him before I do! I *tried* to tell him—" She bit her lip then, ducked her head, and turned toward the window, where she parked her elbows on the narrow sill.

Uh-oh, Aubrey thought. As she watched Sara's face another chill crept up her back, and she wondered why she felt so certain that Sara had almost said something she wasn't supposed to.

"Thank God Mother and Dad are in the middle of the Atlantic." Sara sighed, dragging her fingers through her hair, then glanced at Aubrey. "They don't get TV and newspapers on cruise ships, do they?"

"I don't know," she admitted. "If so, we'll just have to hope your parents are having so much fun they don't have time to keep up with the news."

"Two days," Sara murmured, as she stared blankly out the window. "Forty-eight hours before they dock in Bimini. Oh, God, *please* let this mess be cleaned up by then. They'd be so worried!"

"Do you have any idea what's going on?" Aubrey asked. "Like, what's an LC-15, anyway?"

"Something Jack's been working on." Sara lowered her arms, folded her wrists, and stared at them as she shrugged. "Beyond that, I know as much as you do."

*She's lying.*

Now Aubrey knew it. She knew it just as surely as she knew that she'd have to fast for a day and do ten extra sit-ups and twenty extra leg-lifts for the next week to work off the chocolate mousse and the wine. She knew, not because Sara was a bad actress, but because they'd known each other too long and too well.

"Damnit, I just can't *sit* here!" Sara leaped up and started pacing the floor. "I've got to *do* something!"

"Like what?" Aubrey scooted around to face her and leaned forward with her hands on her knees.

"I don't know." Sara frowned, stopped, and turned toward her. "But I'll think of something."

"Make that *we,*" Aubrey corrected her, "and I suggest we start with trying to figure out where Jack is."

"Where the hell do you think he is? He's hiding." Sara glared at her as if she were the village idiot. "I'm telling you, Bree, those letters the FBI found are phony, faked, cooked up to make Jack look guilty." She waved one hand in the air and started pacing again. "He can't come forward until he can prove he's innocent."

She sounds awfully certain of that, Aubrey thought, but replied matter-of-factly, "That makes sense. So who do you think concocted the letters? And why do you suppose they're trying to frame Jack for espionage?"

"I don't know." Sara shrugged again as she paced past the window seat. "I wish to God I did."

It was another lie. Aubrey knew it instantly by

Sara's refusal to meet her gaze as she turned and walked past her a second time. Aubrey wanted to say to Sara, "I'm on to you." She wanted to, but her lingering suspicion that there had to be a germ of truth somewhere in the "Nightline" report, and that Sara knew it, turned what little natural backbone she had to jelly.

Her lips pursed thoughtfully, Sara came to a halt in front of the window seat. She thrust her hands on her hips and narrowed one eye at Aubrey.

"I wonder," she said slowly, "what Uncle Hugh knows—and what he told the FBI?"

"Uncle Who?" Aubrey asked, rising and following Sara as she made for the telephone on the bar.

"Hugh Lawrence," she explained as she detoured past the cherry wall unit and took a green leather address book out of a drawer. "The man Ted Koppel said Jack was seen with earlier tonight. He's an old friend of my parents."

Pressing the "L" tab, Sara flipped the book open and murmured the number as she crossed the room and lifted the receiver of the pink Princess telephone. Still trailing behind her, Aubrey bit her lip and resisted the sudden urge she felt to take the phone out of Sara's hand, depress the switchhook and say, "Look, I know you know *something,* so why don't you just tell me what it is?" She didn't, though. She just bit her lip harder and watched Sara dial.

"Damn!" Sara slammed the receiver down. "Disconnected—temporarily out of service." She slapped her address book shut, climbed onto one of two maplewood stools before the bar, and frowned.

"Correct me if I'm wrong," Aubrey said, "but doesn't that mean he hasn't paid his bill?"

"That's exactly what it means." Sara's frown deepened. "Until I started getting regular parts, my phone was off more than it was on. Jack's last letter said Uncle Hugh's lab wasn't doing so hot—wait!" She picked up the phone again and dialed long distance information. "That was his home number. I'll bet he pays the lab bill."

"But it's late," Aubrey objected. "Even in California—"

Sara shushed her with a wave and spoke to the operator. Leaning her elbows on the bar, Aubrey listened to the faint ringing she could hear through the receiver as Sara stretched away from it to retrieve her purse from the far end of the bar. No one answered, and Sara's frown returned as she hung up, dug through her purse for a pack of Virginia Slims, and lit one. Her fingers trembled as she drew the cigarette away from her mouth and sighed, blowing smoke through her nose.

"I don't think there's anything we can do tonight," Aubrey said gently. "Why don't you go to bed and get some sleep?"

"I can't sleep," Sara said, staring over the bar at the back wall of her minuscule galley kitchen.

"You could at least rest."

With her head propped on her left hand, Sara glanced at her and smiled. "You're bushed, aren't you? But as always you're too considerate to say, 'For God's sake, Sara, I drove two days to get here, so knock it off already and let's turn in.' "

"I believe the word is *nonassertive* rather than *considerate.*" Aubrey smiled. "But yes, frankly, I'm exhausted."

"I'm sorry, Bree." Sara stubbed out her cigarette in a pink ceramic ashtray. "C'mon, let's make up the sofa."

Removing the cushions, unfolding the hide-a-bed, and putting on fresh sheets took less than fifteen minutes. Afterward, Aubrey suggested a glass of warm skim milk to help them both sleep. Sara opted for cocoa, but changed her mind once Aubrey added up their caloric intake for the evening.

"Low fat or not," Sara said, grimacing at Aubrey with a white-rimmed lip as she pushed her gray stoneware mug away from her, "this is putrid." She shuddered, swung off her stool at the bar, and walked to the coffee table, now pushed against the wall unit. "I'll stick with the vino," she said, lifting the dark green bottle and her goblet as she turned and smiled at Aubrey. "I'm *really* glad you're here, Bree. Good night."

"Me too," she answered with a smile. "Good night, Sara."

As she watched her walk into the bedroom and partly close the door between them, the smile faded from Aubrey's lips and she slid off the bar stool. Carrying her mug with her, she walked to the table beside the hide-a-bed, switched off the pink lamp, then sat on the edge of the cool, clean sheets. With her back to Jack's picture, she sipped her milk and tried to swallow the lump in her throat.

A narrow wedge of pale yellow light spilled across the carpet as she listened to Sara move around her bedroom. Sheets rustled, bedsprings groaned, and glass clinked against glass several times in rapid succession. In the half-dark Aubrey smiled. At least she's gotten some class in her old age, she thought, remembering the countless gallons of Boone's Farm strawberry wine Sara had chugged straight from the bottle in college.

Oh, God. Remembering was a mistake. The lump in her throat swelled and a sharp pang stabbed Aubrey between her ribs. She took a deep breath, drained her mug, but it didn't help—the lump was still there—and so were the memories. She tried to push them out of her mind but they wouldn't go away. She tried to think about her doctoral thesis and thought about Jack instead; she tried to think about the Peterson School where she taught and thought about Jack instead.

In desperation, she tried to summon an image of her high school library, the only refuge she'd had from an otherwise painful adolescence, but her brain just wouldn't cooperate. It refused to place her there, in that carpeted new wing filled with low, modern tables and fresh leather bindings still smelling of ink; instead, her mind planted itself firmly before the reception lounge window in her dormitory at Stephens, forcing her to look out at Jack in a navy blazer and gray slacks and Sara in her cap and gown, both laughing as they'd wedged themselves into his red Volkswagen Bug.

It was graduation day, the biggest day of Aubrey's life, made larger and more important by Jack's arrival from MIT to drive Sara and her to commencement. Only Jack hadn't thought about the car, but Aubrey had known the second she'd come down the steps with Sara that the only way they'd get her into the minuscule backseat was with a shoehorn. The bubble of joy in her breast had burst and she'd tripped over nothing as she'd seen the flicker of dismay, the quick "oh-*God!*" glance he'd thrown at the car as he'd straightened off the fender he'd been leaning against. Aubrey had wrenched away from Sara's hand on her sleeve then, had hissed at her not to wait because she was a nervous wreck and had to go back upstairs to throw up—or something else equally stupid, she couldn't remember exactly what she'd said—as she'd whirled around, flown back up the steps, ducked into the lounge, and stood there at the window, clenching her mortarboard to her chest and sobbing as she'd watched them drive away.

Soft, muffled sounds—Sara, crying into her pillow—drifted out of the bedroom. Drawing a deep, shuddery breath, Aubrey pulled herself back to the present, blinked around the now dark living room, and listened to Sara cry. Of all the lovely memories she had, of all the times Jack had come down to Stephens with a present for Sara and one for her too, of all the holidays she'd spent with the Drapers on their farm in Ithaca, when Jack had taken them ice skating or horseback riding—why in the world had she remembered *that?* Why hadn't she remembered the full-on-the-mouth kiss Jack had given her after commencement, or the three times he'd danced with her at their graduation party that night?

Sara's tears tapered off to occasional feathery sighs. Is she thinking what I'm thinking, Aubrey wondered, is she crying because the thing that frightens her most is that no one knows where Jack is? Is she wondering where he is, if he's all right—

A stifled sob burst past Aubrey's lips, and she

clapped both hands over her mouth as her shoulders heaved and tears spilled down her cheeks. Oh, God, what if Sara was right? What if the letters were faked, what if someone were trying to frame Jack for something, what if he'd found out, confronted him, what if he'd had a gun—

"Bree?" Sara called softly from the bedroom doorway, her voice thick in the darkness. "Are you all right?"

Hurriedly, Aubrey dragged her right sleeve across her face, swallowed hard, and cleared her throat. "Y-yes," she answered, wincing and biting her lip at the telltale tremor in her voice.

"So is Jack, so don't worry," Sara said gently. "We've only got to get through these next two days, and then everything will be all right." She paused, then added, "Trust me."

Oh, sure, Aubrey thought, trust you while you lie to me some more. She rolled into bed on her stomach and gathered the pillow into a soft mound to hug into her chest. She lay there staring at the back of the sofa, wondering what Sara would tell Mr. and Mrs. Draper when they arrived in Bimini, and if she hadn't fallen asleep just then, she would've gotten up and asked Sara.

# Chapter Three

A LONG steady buzz, like a yellow jacket bumping against a window, stirred Aubrey from her wine-clouded sleep. At first, still dazed and groaning, she thought the source of the clamor was inside her head. But as she pushed her thick auburn hair out of her face and blearily cracked one eye, she recognized the sound of someone impatiently ringing the bell.

"Jack—" she murmured breathlessly and bolted, wide-awake, to her feet.

At that same moment Sara came tearing out of the bedroom, tying a flowered kimono over her lavender nightie. She shot Aubrey a hopeful smile and beat her to the door by two steps.

"Who's there?" Sara asked into the intercom.

"FBI, Miss Draper. We'd like to speak with you."

Disappointment sent Aubrey's heart thudding to the soles of her feet, followed instantly by panic which sent it rocketing back to her throat. The two women exchanged a wide-eyed glance.

"Just a moment, please," Sara answered as she caught Aubrey's elbow and tugged her away from the door. "Wipe that startled-doe look off your face, Bree," she whispered. "They just want to ask us some questions." She squeezed her arm reassuringly with fingers that were only trembling slightly and gave her a shove toward the bedroom. "Now go get a robe out of my closet before they come up."

Because she'd always done as she was told, Aubrey nodded and hurriedly headed for the bedroom, her heart yammering in the hollow of her throat. From Sara's room, as she tugged a blue cotton robe off a hanger, she heard a knock, followed by the chain rattling against the wooden molding and the door scraping open. Holding down the hems of her pajama sleeves with her fingers, she slid into the lightweight wrapper and heard the quiet drone of voices fill the living room. Listening intently she tied the belt around her waist, hastily raked her fingers through her hair to sort out some of the sleepy tangles, and scurried toward the door.

In the threshold Aubrey paused and hesitantly peeked around the doorframe into the living room. Sitting sideways on the arm of the hide-a-bed, her fingers laced loosely together in her lap, Sara looked deep in conversation with two men who were standing near the front door. Dressed in business suits, one was dark-haired, the other fair, and both were tall and well built. To Aubrey, whose experience with the FBI was limited to watching late-night reruns of the television program by the same name, neither of them looked much like Efrem Zimbalist Jr.; with their wide shoulders and muscled chests straining the fabric of their well-tailored dark suits, they looked more like NFL linebackers dressed to pay a call on their accountant.

"I haven't heard from Jack," Sara was saying, "in, oh, weeks, I'd say. We're not terribly close, you see. We live on opposite coasts."

She said it calmly and straight-faced as her right hand rose to her throat and fumbled absently with the gold locket and chain around her neck. Watching her, Aubrey marveled at her friend's natural acting ability, but suddenly she was hit with the seriousness of the game. With her hand clamped firmly over her mouth, it was all she could do to keep from shrieking, "For God's sake, Sara, don't *lie* to the FBI."

The dark man, by far the burlier of the two, nodded and jotted something in a small black notebook. Standing to his left and slightly behind him, his blond-haired partner shifted his weight to one hip, folded his arms, and glanced toward the bedroom. His cool, Nordic blue eyes settled on Aubrey in the doorway, and a sliver of ice chilled her spine.

"Miss Nichols?" he asked.

"Y-y-yes?" she blurted, her voice a high, nervous squeak that drew a relax-will-you frown from Sara. Clearing her tight, dry throat, she straightened her robe, then looked back anxiously at the two agents. "Pardon, me, I-I have a cold."

She hadn't meant to stammer, but the tension in the room was unbearable. Sara's frown, glued to Aubrey's face, hardened into deep lines; *careful*, it cautioned her as Aubrey felt cold perspiration trickle down her rib cage. Taking a deep breath, she forced herself to smile.

"Yes, Miss Nichols." The dark, burly man

turned toward her, unsmiling. "Are you acquainted with Jack Draper?"

"Acquainted?" she repeated as if trying to discern the meaning of the word. Pressing one hand to her chest, she felt a bubble of panic begin to swell behind her breastbone. "Oh, yes, I—well, yes, he's Sara's brother."

One corner of Sara's mouth lifted in a no-kidding smirk. The bubble in Aubrey's chest tightened, and her trembly fingers knotted around the left lapel of her robe.

"Don't be nervous, Miss Nichols," the dark man said, lowering his head to write something in his notebook. "This is only routine. When was the last time you saw Dr. Draper?"

"Ohhh—" Her voice warbled unsteadily and she cleared her throat again. "Pardon me. It's been—years, really—*years.* Since we graduated from college, right, Sara?"

"Oh, no," she corrected her casually, "you've seen Jack since then. Don't you remember my cousin Emily's wedding three years ago?"

For ten awful seconds, Aubrey couldn't even remember the names of her own cousins, let alone Sara's. She stared at her best friend, panic-stricken, until Sara drew her eyebrows together in a familiar gesture. *C'mon, Bree, back me up. . . .* Finally, Aubrey's brain and her mouth meshed gears.

"Oh, yes," she gushed, strongly suspecting that she sounded as confused as she felt. "Oh, yes, Emily's wedding. I guess Jack *was* there, wasn't he?"

"Yes, Aubrey." Sara nodded slowly but firmly,

as if talking to a child. "You danced with him *four* times at the reception."

"I did?" she asked blankly.

The dark man glanced at the goblet of wine Aubrey had left on the coffee table the night before, then at his partner, and closed his notebook. He tucked it inside his lapel pocket, withdrew a brown leather wallet, and extracted a small white card from an inside window.

"That's all for now, Miss Draper," he said, holding the card out to Sara as she rose to take it. "Please call me if you hear from your brother."

"You bet." She smiled and tucked the card in her kimono pocket without reading it.

The two men looked at each other once again, said good morning, and left. Closing the door quickly behind them, Sara fastened the chain, then turned toward Aubrey.

"Oh, God, Sara, I'm *sorry!*" Aubrey wailed, covering her face with her hands to avoid the murderous glare on Sara's face. "I was so nervous I couldn't think—"

"Don't be sorry!" Sara cried, rushing toward her and throwing her arms out wide. "You were wonderful, Bree!"

"I was?" Bewildered, Aubrey peeked up from her cupped palms and blinked at her.

Laughing, Sara swooped her into a quick hug, spun her in a half-circle, and then rushed for the window. Still dazed, Aubrey swept her hair out of her face then followed her to the raspberry chintz window seat, where Sara was now kneeling and peering through the beige open-weave drapes. Leaning over her shoulder, Aubrey looked down at the sidewalk and saw the two men stop outside the building. They exchanged a few words, then moved toward a dark blue sedan double-parked on the opposite side of the street. Neither of them glanced up at Sara's apartment.

"Oh, you little genius!" Sara chortled gleefully as she watched them get into the car and drive away. "You ought to get a Tony for that performance!"

"So who was performing?" Aubrey asked, wiping her hands on her robe again. "I was scared out of my wits, tripping over my tongue—"

"Yes, I know, and you convinced them that they were wasting their time on two ditsy women."

Pivoting off the window seat, Sara grinned and pinched Aubrey's cheeks affectionately; then, chuckling and rubbing her hands together, she started for the kitchen. More bewildered than ever, and rapidly becoming fed up at being the only one who didn't know what was going on, Aubrey traipsed after her indignantly.

"Wait just a cotton-pickin' minute, Sara," she said firmly. "What if they *didn't* believe us? What if they come back? And why did you lie about not hearing from Jack? You just got the locket from him yesterday by express mail. You told me the package arrived just before I did."

"What was I supposed to do?" Sara retorted as she swung a copper tea kettle onto the front burner of the range and switched on the gas. "*Help* them?"

"Did it ever occur to you," Aubrey asked, balling her fists on her hips as she stopped in the small walkspace between the counter and the wall and frowned at Sara, "that cooperating with the FBI could help Jack? If he *is* being framed for trying to sell this LC-15 thing to some other government, then he's in big trouble, Sara, and I think he needs all the help he can get."

"I'm *trying* to help him." Sara wheeled away from the stove, rested her left hand against it, and glared at Aubrey.

"Not by lying to the FBI you aren't!"

"Oh, for God's sake, Bree!" she cried angrily and punched the rangetop with the heel of her hand. "Those two goons were *not*—" Sara bit off her sentence, pressing her lips together, and tried to push past her. " 'Scuse me, I'm going to be late for rehearsal."

This time, Aubrey refused to do as she was told. Firmly lifting her chin, she stepped in front of Sara.

"Those two goons were not *what?*"

"Oh, nothing—" Sara waved one hand dismissively and tried to cut around her again. "Just forget—"

"No." Aubrey flung out her left arm, pressing her palm against the wall to block her path. "I'm not going to forget this."

"Bree, I'm *late,*" she snapped impatiently and tried to sidle past her a third time.

"I don't care, Sara." Flinging her right arm against the other side of the walkspace, Aubrey this time planted her whole body in front of Sara to cut her off.

"*Look,* Bree—" Sara began sharply, then caught her bottom lip between her teeth. "Look," she tried again, her voice softer now. "There's no point talking about this. I'm probably full of it, anyway, and I don't want to scare you—"

"It's too late for that," Aubrey interrupted. "I *am* scared and I want some answers."

For a long moment Sara just stared at her, then she sighed, leaning back against the side of the stove and folding her arms at her waist. "Okay, okay," she said irritably. "I don't think those two guys were real FBI agents."

"Why not? Didn't they have badges?"

"Oh, sure, but they flashed them so fast I never got a good look. And there was just something"—she paused and her eyebrows and the corners of her mouth puckered—"something not quite *right* about them, you know what I mean?"

"Boy, do I," Aubrey agreed, shivering as she remembered the chill the fair-haired man's eyes had given her. "So if they weren't FBI, who do you think they were?"

"I don't know. And furthermore," Sara added emphatically as she tried to wiggle past Aubrey, "I don't *want* to know."

"Well, I do." Aubrey reinforced her palms firmly against the wall and the cabinet. "Let's check the number on the card he gave you against the phone book. If it isn't the same, I suggest we call the *real* FBI."

"No," Sara said, her voice stony.

"But, *Sa*-ra—"

"No!" she thundered suddenly, and shoved Aubrey out of her way.

Flattened against the wall in her wake, Aubrey turned in time to see the hem of Sara's kimono disappear around the jamb into the bedroom. Sara slammed the door so hard that the Hummel figurines on the cherry wall unit trembled. A second later the lock clicked and a slow, hot flush washed up Aubrey's throat.

"I think that means mind your own business, old girl," Aubrey said out loud to herself as she turned into the kitchen and pulled the steaming, shrieking teakettle off the burner.

On the second shelf of the tiny, curtain-draped pantry she found a gray ceramic pot and a metal tin filled with Lipton tea bags. She tore three out of their paper wrappers, dropped them in the pot, then filled it with boiling water. While the tea steeped Aubrey moved to the counter behind the bar, leaning her elbows on it and listening to the muted roar of the shower in the bathroom.

If Jack were innocent, if someone were trying to frame him, then Sara's opposition to calling the FBI made no sense. If, however, he were guilty—and if Sara knew it—then her vehemence made a *lot* of sense.

That Sara knew something, Aubrey had no doubt. The question was, *what*—and what was Aubrey going to do about it?

What if the two men came back? What if they weren't real FBI agents? The Mary Stewart novels Aubrey had read and loved raced through her mind, and her hands began to tremble. Oh, God, she thought nervously, things like that only happened in fiction—didn't they?

Vowing never to read another suspense novel as long as she lived, Aubrey walked back to the stove and poured herself a cup of tea. There was no low-calorie sweetener in the pantry, so she settled for a dash of skim milk and carried her mug with her into the living room. She'd just finished folding up the hide-a-bed, replacing the coffee table in front of it, and washing her sticky wineglass from the night before, when Sara, in a calf-length striped wrap skirt and a coordinating raspberry blouse, came out of the bedroom.

Pretending not to notice her, Aubrey wrung out the dishcloth and diligently wiped the countertops and the bar. From the corner of her eye she watched Sara swing an oversized beige leather shoulder bag onto the sofa and walk toward her with a rectangular white box in her hand.

"Peace offering," she said as she swung up on one of the barstools and held the box out to her.

Tugging the dishtowel she'd flung there off her shoulder, Aubrey dried her hands, looked up at Sara, and took the box. She was smiling, and though she'd very carefully applied her makeup, dark smudges still showed beneath her eyes.

"I'm not angry, Sara," Aubrey told her quietly.

"Neither am I. So come on, open it."

Aubrey did and caught her breath. On a bed of cotton lay an exquisitely lovely green marble fountain pen. It was a very old Sheaffer, its brass clip tarnished, and her fingers trembled again, with excitement now, as she lifted it and scrutinized the nib.

"Oh, Sara," she breathed. "Where did you find this? It's in mint condition."

"In a junk store while I was hunting props. Do you like it?"

"You shouldn't have." Aubrey frowned at her. "It must've cost a fortune."

"Nope, only five bucks. Oops!" Sara clapped a hand over her mouth, then grinned at her sheepishly. "How rude to tell you the price."

"That's cheap." Aubrey rolled the pen in her

hand and admired the green pearlized finish. "Obviously, they didn't know what they had."

"Most people just write with fountain pens, Bree. So what do you think, Madame Collector? Is it worth anything?"

"Could be, I'm not sure," she said as she hurried around the bar. "Let me check my book—"

"Later, okay? I've got to scoot for rehearsal."

Already halfway through the bedroom door, Aubrey turned around in time to see Sara swing her bag off the hide-a-bed and over her shoulder. "Kind of early, isn't it?" she asked.

"I thought I'd walk around for a while before rehearsal starts . . ." Sara paused, smiling crookedly as she tucked her hands in her skirt pockets. ". . . and think about calling the FBI. The *real* FBI."

"Oh, *thank* you, Sara," Aubrey sighed gratefully.

"I said *think,*" she reminded her with a raised finger, but smiled wider.

"I know, I know," Aubrey agreed quickly. "Take all the time you need—just remember we're in this together."

"I won't forget." Sara wrinkled her nose at her and hooked her left thumb around the strap of her purse as she walked to the door. "I was going to save the pen for Christmas," she said as she unfastened the chain and opened the door. "But I decided to give it to you now just in case."

"Just in case *what?*"

"Just in case," Sara repeated as she pivoted in the threshold and grimaced, "I get hit by a truck, dummy." She looked at the ceiling, shook her head, then closed the door.

"Thank you for bringing her to her senses, Lord," Aubrey murmured fervently as she scurried across the room and refastened the locks. "Oh, thank you, thank you, *thank* you."

# Chapter Four

SIGHING again with relief, Aubrey carried the pen to the window seat, sat with her legs folded beneath her, and lifted the drape. She held the Sheaffer next to the glass and watched its pearl finish warm and glow in the sunlight. With her elbow bent on the narrow sill, Aubrey leaned against the wooden molding behind her and looked down at the sidewalk.

Almost directly below her, Sara stood talking to Sam. While she chattered the doorman emptied a half-gallon milk jug full of water over the scraggly little tree that grew on the parkway in front of the building. Ah, Aubrey thought, smiling as she leaned her elbow on the sill and her chin on the heel of her hand. She was glad to know it was Sam who took care of the struggling maple.

Watching Sara now as she wagged her fingers at Sam, then thrust her hands in her skirt pockets and struck off down the sidewalk toward the corner, Aubrey smiled again. Despite her claim to the contrary, she knew darn well that Sara had been furious with her. But that was Sara. One minute she'd shriek at you and the next she'd hug you.

*Mercurial* was Aubrey's favorite word to describe her best friend's personality. Jack, however, always called his younger sister pouty and moody. Well, maybe she was, just a little, Aubrey admitted, but she was funny and fun, spontaneous, vivacious—all the things Aubrey had always wanted to be but never had been.

Long ago, she'd given up hoping that Sara would rub off on her, that somehow, by osmosis maybe, she'd absorb some of her vitality. Years ago she'd resigned herself to the fact that one of them had to be sensible, one of them had to keep both feet on the ground, one of them had to be practical and plain. Sure, it was a dirty job, she thought, the corners of her mouth puckering wryly as she watched Sara jaywalk near the middle of the block, but somebody had to—

Suddenly Aubrey's smile vanished as she saw a tall blond man in a dark suit duck between two parked cars and follow Sara across the street. Shooting up on her knees, she thrust the drape aside and pressed her nose to the sun-warmed glass. The memory of gilt hair and blue eyes as pale and frigid as a fjord made her heart skip a beat, and her fingers closed like talons on the curtain. Oh, please God, no, she prayed.

Waiting for the light to change at the corner, Sara abruptly turned around just as the man approached her from behind. Together they moved back from the curb, faced each other off, then Sara wheeled away from him as the light changed. She crossed the street hurriedly and turned right. The blond man remained on the curb watching her until she'd walked out of Aubrey's view; then as the light changed again he half-ran across the intersection and walked straight ahead.

Trembling with relief, Aubrey sagged back on her heels and sighed. A flash of light below—sunlight reflecting off a windshield—caught her attention, and she looked down at the street in time to see a dark blue sedan pull away from the curb and accelerate up the block.

"Oh, God, *no,*" she moaned out loud, her fingers gripping the edge of the sill as she shot up on her knees, pressed her face to the window, and watched the car stop at the corner.

When the light changed, the blue sedan turned right, but Aubrey's cry of alarm died in her throat when she saw the one-way sign mounted above the traffic signal. Flushing a bright crimson, she pushed herself off the window seat and carried the Sheaffer into the bedroom.

That's it, she swore silently. No more suspense novels. Not *ever.*

She lifted the smallest of her powder blue suitcases onto Sara's unmade brass bed, raised the lid, and withdrew from the taffeta pocket a copy of *The Official Pen Fancier's Guide.* Sitting on the rumpled sheets, she pored through its pages of photographs. It took her nearly twenty minutes, but at last she identified Sara's gift as a 1930 Sheaffer Lifetime pen. The lustrous green marble finish was called emerald pearl. She repeated the name softly several times as she replaced the pen in its box, and then tucked it inside the zippered pocket of her burgundy briefcase-style shoulder bag.

What a lovely addition to her collection, she thought, smiling as she envisioned the glass-doored oak wall cabinet she'd had specially made to showcase her antique fountain pens. Thinking about the collection was a mistake, however, and her smile faded as she tucked her purse on the floor between a small pink chintz chair and Sara's walnut dresser. She turned hurriedly toward the bathroom, detouring past the linen closet for a towel and washcloth, as she tried to shake the image of the case and the tan tortoiseshell Parker in the top row that Jack had sent her when she'd earned her master's in American literature.

There'd been a note with it, scrawled on a plain beige note card in his large, firm handwriting. For a long time it had sat propped against the marble pen stand on her desk, but one day she'd slid it inside an empty manila envelope with old Christmas cards she'd saved, carried it to the attic of her small white clapboard house, and deliberately lost it there three years ago, when the letter from Sara announcing Jack's engagement had arrived. The words were still burned into her soul, however, and she read the note again in her mind as she stripped off Sara's robe and her fat-jams and stepped into the shower: "Don't just put this away someplace, Dumpling. Use it—it works as well as it ever did—and think of me whenever you grade a paper with it. Always, Jack."

The tortoiseshell Parker had gone into the case that same afternoon. It was there still. Though it did, in fact, work as well as it ever did, her silly, someday fantasies about Jack simply wouldn't work thereafter—despite the breakup of his engagement six months later.

Since then, Aubrey hadn't once daydreamed about him. Not once in all that time had she savored the memory of his graduation kiss or dancing with him at Emily Draper's wedding. He'd been very strange then, oddly aloof, almost disdainful. She'd written it off to his recent "unengagement," but still it had hurt, and it convinced her beyond a doubt that he'd never cared for her, that he never would, and that his doting, brotherly affection for her had never been anything but that—brotherly.

Still, old dreams die hard, and Aubrey sighed as she shut off the water, pulled back the hot-pink shower curtain, and remembered the surge in her pulse she'd felt when she'd read the letter Sara had sent her just three weeks ago. Maybe, just *maybe,* she'd written, Jack would be at the farm for the Fourth. Always firm in her resolve, Aubrey had then taken the money she'd put aside for a furnace and spent every cent on a new wardrobe, a closetful of stylish size-ten outfits that Jack, considering the circumstances, would probably never see.

Unless she wore the cream linen suit to his arraignment, she thought as she unpacked a pair of cuffed clamdiggers and a sleeveless lightweight aquamarine sweater that matched the windowpane check in the calf-length pants. *Pedal pushers* they'd called them when she was in high school, when she'd been too fat to wear them. And the navy jersey shirtwaist with the white-piped cap sleeves would look appropriately somber in the courtroom when the judge sentenced him—

Tears threatened behind her eyelids, and Aubrey jerked off the towel wrapped around her body. Burying her face in the damp terry-cloth pile, she drew several shaky deep breaths. This is the United States of America, she reminded herself, where a man is innocent until proven guilty; yet why was she being so quick to judge? Could it be that seeing Jack carted off to jail would be easier on her ego and her resurfaced hopes than facing another rejection?

No, no, and *no.* Refusing to give credence to the ridiculous notion, Aubrey dressed hurriedly. Slipping her feet into canvas espadrilles, she fastened triangular aquamarine earrings to her pierced lobes and eased a bracelet that matched them over her right wrist. With Sara at rehearsal, she decided, this morning would be a good time to find her way to the NYU campus. She brushed her thick auburn hair out around her shoulders, picked up her purse, and withdrew a small leather notebook from a side compartment as she left the bedroom.

In the kitchen, she made herself another cup of tea and, in the margin of the page where she'd taken down the directions to NYU that Sara had given her yesterday, she made a note to buy low-calorie sweetener. She sat at the bar, read the directions carefully three times, and frowned. Even with her city map she doubted she could get there in her red Camaro without getting lost at least six times. Why hadn't she asked Sara about bus or train connections? Maybe Sam the doorman could tell her.

With her purse slung over her left shoulder, Aubrey was three steps shy of the door and just reaching out to grasp the knob with her right hand when the intercom buzzed. *Jack,* she thought instantly—then remembered the blond man who'd followed Sara down the block. Her heart yammered loudly in her ears, and she chewed her bottom lip as the bell rang again.

Although her first instinct was not to answer it, the possibility—remote as it was—that Jack could be downstairs waiting gave her courage enough to ask in a wary, voice, "Who is it?"

"Felix O'Malley. I'm with the FBI. May I speak with you please?"

Oh, God, *no!* Biting her lip nervously, Aubrey clenched the strap of her purse in her left hand and swept her right hand through her hair. Now what? She'd already let him know she was here. . . .

"Do you have a chain on the door, Miss?"

"Y-yes," she stammered.

"Leave it on but open the door and I'll show you my badge."

"All right." Sounds safe enough—*I hope*—Aubrey thought. When he got to the door, she did as instructed with cold, clumsy fingers and peered through the small space between frame and door. The laminated ID and badge certainly looked official, but there were all kinds of places—especially in a city the size of New York—where, for a fee, you could have documents forged that could fool experts.

Felix O'Malley resembled William Frawley more than Efrem Zimbalist Jr. Despite his slouched, pudgy physique stuffed into a heat-rumpled green tweed suit, his shoulders were wide and his chest deep. He certainly wasn't in the same class as the two linebackers, but he was a tall, strong-looking man despite his paunch, and the memory of the blond man tailing Sara was fresh enough in Aubrey's mind to make her cautious.

"I'm not Sara Draper," she told him through the door. "She isn't here right now."

"You are—?"

"Aubrey Nichols. I'm just a friend."

He smiled and tucked his identification back in his suitcoat.

"When do you expect Miss Draper?"

"I don't know. She went out"—she hesitated, wondering how much she should say, then finished —"for a walk."

"I see." He frowned slightly. "Do you know her brother, Jack?"

"Yes," she said simply, and his frown deepened.

"Do you know if Miss Draper has seen or heard from him recently?"

"Oh, no," she replied quickly, then hastily added Sara's lie: "They're not terribly close, you see. They live on opposite coasts."

"Yes, I know that." He reached inside his coat again, took out the same black case, extracted a card, and wedged it through the door. "Would you please have Miss Draper call me when she returns?"

"Yes, I will." Aubrey pinched the card out of his fingers, pushed the door shut, refastened the locks, and turned her back against it.

Holding her breath, she leaned there, counting silently until she heard his footsteps move away. On *fifty* the floorboards creaked just outside the door; on *sixty-five* she heard the elevator open at the end of the hall. She'd counted rapidly, still it seemed to Aubrey that it had taken him an awfully long time to walk away.

Shaking inside and out, she hurried to the cherry wall unit, opened a bottom door, and took out the thick, heavy telephone directory. With icy, damp fingers, she turned to the United States Government listings, used the card as a guide, and drew it down a long column. She stopped it below the number given for the FBI and compared it to the one on O'Malley's card.

It was the same.

# Chapter Five

WITH her heart beating in the back of her throat, Aubrey slammed the directory shut and leaned her half-balled fists against it. *Oh, God.* She'd lied to a real FBI agent.

No, wait a minute, she thought quickly, trying to rationalize away the panic bubbling in her chest again. She hadn't really lied, she'd just omitted parts of the truth. Was it technically the same? Oh, damn, what if she got arrested for lying to them and her *mother* found out?

She could see her petite, wrenlike parent now, could hear her saying in her firm, quiet voice, "Well, Aubrey, I'm grateful for one thing at least—your father isn't here to see this." And then, of course, she'd go on and on about Sara: "A sweet girl, really, but so *flighty . . .*"

"Oh, God," she moaned, pressing her unsteady fingers to her mouth as she whirled away from the telephone directory and leaned shakily against the wall unit. "What am I going to *do?*"

She knew what she wanted to do—pack her bags and run like hell for Springfield. But she couldn't do that—she couldn't run out on Sara. That was that. But what would Sara do?

To begin with, Aubrey realized, Sara wouldn't just stand here having an anxiety attack. She'd put the phone book away—well, no, truthfully, Sara wouldn't bother, but Aubrey replaced it in the wall unit anyway—then she'd light a cigarette probably, pace the floor, and think.

Only, Aubrey realized as she shut the cabinet door and turned around, there really wasn't time to think. Felix O'Malley was legit, which meant Sara had been right about the two men who'd interviewed them earlier. What had she called them?

*Goons,* that was it. The word sent a chill up Aubrey's back. There were two goons looking for Jack, two goons who'd asked Sara to contact them if she heard from him.

Chewing nervously on her bottom lip, Aubrey replayed the tape her brain had made of the interview as she moved to the bar to finish her tea. She watched the dark man glance first at the wineglass, then at his partner, close his notebook, hand Sara the card, and glance at his partner again. She remembered the subtle lift of the dark man's right eyebrow and the icy, calculating smile that had barely turned the corners of the blond man's thin mouth.

They hadn't believed them. She knew it now, and she wondered if that was why they'd hung around, if that was why the blond man had followed Sara to the corner. Was he out there still with his dark, unsmiling partner?

It didn't matter. Whether he was or wasn't, Sara had to be told about O'Malley.

Quickly, Aubrey drained her mug, put it in the sink, ran water in it, then hurried to the wall unit where she'd left her purse. As she raced for the door she unzipped it, tugged out her notebook and key ring, and made sure she had the apartment key Sara had given her yesterday. Opening the front door, she stepped out into the red-carpeted hall, made sure the lock was on, and firmly shut the door behind her.

In the elevator, she looked in her notebook for the name and address of the theater where Sara's play was in rehearsal. When the doors opened on the first floor, she cut rapidly down the short expanse of corridor to the lobby, where Sam the doorman stood in his gray uniform by the double glass doors. He turned at the sound of her footsteps on the red and white tiled floor, smiled, and touched his fingertips to the bill of his cap.

"Good morning, Miss Nichols."

"Morning, Sam," she answered as she showed him the address Sara had jotted in her notebook. "Could you tell me how to get here, please?"

"Miss Draper's theater?" He looked up at her and she nodded. "You could drive, but you'd never find a place to park in Chelsea. I suggest the bus, down Broadway to Eighth Avenue, or could I call you a cab?"

"I can't afford a cab, Sam. Which bus should I take?"

He told her and directed her to the nearest stop. Thanking him as he held the door open, she stepped out into the already hot, humid morning. While she strode hurriedly down the sidewalk following Sam's directions, Aubrey dodged pedestrians and glanced at her Timex. Eleven forty-five.

Aubrey lifted her heavy hair off her perspiring neck as she came to a halt at the bus stop where two plump women in flowered dresses waited. She paced idly back and forth, hoping the glances she shot up and down the block looked casual. She didn't see either the blond man or the dark man.

Within five minutes the bus arrived; she boarded and found a seat near the front. Clenching her purse on her lap, she listened to the rapid, staccato conversations around her and tried not to think. She might as well have tried not to breathe. Turning slightly toward the window, she stared hard at the crowded sidewalks and the buildings that grew taller and closer together as the bus neared the heart of Manhattan. She saw several newsstands and wished she'd thought to buy a paper. Maybe there'd be an article about Jack.

She thought so hard about not thinking that she missed the stop Sam had told her would let her off closest to Sara's theater. At the next one she got off and doubled back two blocks to Eighteenth Street, ducking and weaving her way along the people-clogged sidewalk to the locked front of the theater. *Terrific.* Giving the bar across the heavy glass door a disgusted tug, Aubrey turned away from it. Oh, well, she thought, there had to be another entrance someplace—all she had to do was find it.

Behind her, she heard metal clink against wood and pivoted on her right foot. A small, thin man in khaki workpants and shirt pushed the door open and leaned outside. A fat ring of keys dangled from the lock.

"Help you, miss?" he asked.

"Oh, yes," Aubrey sighed, relieved. "I'd like to see Sara Draper, please. She's in the cast of—"

Her mind went blank; oh, hell, she didn't even know the name of the play.

"I dunno . . ." The little man eyed her dubiously. "Mr. Parsons, the director, isn't crazy about visitors."

"Oh, I won't disturb the rehearsal," she promised. "I'll just wait quietly until they finish." She waited, but when his expression didn't change, she added pleadingly, "Honest."

"Well . . ." He paused again, then sighed and pushed the door open wider. "Okay. But if he sees you and throws a fit, I didn't let you in."

"Thanks." She smiled and sidled past him into the lobby.

She noticed nothing of its decor except the dingy hardwood floor that echoed her footsteps and those of the custodian as he led her across it. Outside the auditorium door he shushed her, eased it open, and ushered her inside with a whispered "Slide into the first row back here, and maybe he won't see you."

Mouthing a thank-you, Aubrey eased past him. Blackness enfolded her, and she stood in the carpeted aisle, blinking at the stage and the several figures milling around it until her eyes adjusted to the darkness. They seemed miles away from her, and once she could make out the dim shapes of the seats, she settled noiselessly into one, its ancient upholstery creaking beneath her.

Confident that the director would never know she was there, Aubrey slid her purse to the floor, leaned forward, and scanned the stage again. There were four women standing and sitting around the bare, makeshift set, but Sara wasn't one of them. Where the hell is she? Aubrey wondered, raising her left wrist close to her face and peering at her watch as a deep voice, sharply edged with exasperation, echoed her thought from the stage.

"Where the hell's Sara? She's forty-five minutes late. Somebody call her apartment, will you?"

"We did already, Sid, twice," came a bored reply from somewhere to the right of the stage. "No answer."

The first voice spat an obscenity, and Aubrey glanced up as a tall, aesthetically thin man with a full dark beard dragged one hand through his thin, curly hair and paced the stage apron. The director, she thought, and shrank lower in her seat.

A half-hour later—Aubrey knew the time precisely because she strained her eyes almost every five minutes to read the face of her Timex—Sid stopped pacing. He wheeled, glaring, toward the auditorium, and Aubrey slid even lower on her spine.

"Elsbeth," he snapped as he turned back to his cast. "Read Sara's lines, too, will you? We can't wait all day."

They did, in fact, wait all day for Sara, but Aubrey didn't. At two o'clock, her tailbone as numb as her brain, she crept out of her seat. Four hours. It had been a good four hours since Sara had left the apartment. Where in God's name was she? Though Aubrey had been trying since twelve-thirty, she still couldn't shake the memory of that blond man hurrying after Sara and the feeling of dread that the picture stirred in the pit of her stomach.

The bright afternoon sun streaming through

the doors into the lobby hurt her eyes, and she blinked back frightened tears as she leaned one hand against the wall. Don't cry, Aubrey told herself, don't cry, you don't have time. You've got to *do* something. Sounded good, the only problem was, she couldn't think of anything to do *but* cry; so she did, softly, sagging against the wall on her shoulder, her right hand over her mouth, her left arm curled around her waist.

"Miss Nichols?"

The sob in her throat caught there as she spun around and faced Felix O'Malley. His green suit had more wrinkles and creases than it had had earlier, and his fair, graying eyebrows knotted over the wide bridge of his nose.

"Why are you crying?" he asked gently.

"The—ah—" She smudged her cheek with the back of her hand, tried to laugh, and sighed shakily instead. "The play is s-so sad."

"I think the director would be very unhappy to hear that." He withdrew a clean white handkerchief from his lapel pocket and handed it to her. "It's a comedy."

Her sobs froze in her throat and her heart began to pound. Over the white linen rectangle that she'd hastily raised to her tear-streaked face, she stared wide-eyed at O'Malley.

"Oh, yes, I-I know," she stammered quickly, "and it's just s-so sad that the lines aren't working, isn't it? I-I mean, I think it could be really f-funny—"

"Where's Sara Draper, Miss Nichols?"

Though he'd interrupted her, his voice was still gentle. For the span of two seconds, Aubrey tottered on the verge of wailing "I don't know!" and throwing herself against his rumpled shirtfront. She nearly did, then remembered the admonition she'd given Sara that morning: "Don't forget, we're in this together." She remembered, too, Sara's fury at her suggestion that they call the FBI, and she bit back her urge to confess. Not yet, she cautioned herself—give Sara a little more time.

"I don't know," she told him truthfully as she sniffled and wiped her face. "I wish I *did,*" she went on, hoping she sounded genuinely irritated. "She dragged me all the way down here to meet her and then she doesn't show up."

"Is that like her? Does she often forget rehearsals and meetings with her friends?"

"It's a miracle when she remembers." Aubrey tried to laugh again and this time almost made it. "But that's Sara. The artistic personality, you know."

"Funny," he said quietly. "Her director says she's very conscientious, very dependable. He's quite concerned that she's missed rehearsal."

"She certainly has him fooled, doesn't she?" She smiled weakly, gave her damp eyes a last dab, then refolded the handkerchief and offered it to him. "Thank you, Mr. O'Malley."

"Keep it." He smiled back. "I'll be around."

"Oh," she said, wincing inwardly at the dismay she heard in her voice. "I'll wash it then," she added hurriedly and tucked it in her purse as she started away from him.

She'd taken no more than five steps when his voice stopped her. "Miss Nichols?"

Deep breath and *big* smile, she told herself, forcing the corners of her mouth up as she turned around. "Yes?"

"You do know why I want to talk to Sara, don't you?"

"You want to know if she's heard from Jack, but I already told you—"

"I remember what you told me." The gentleness had gone from his voice. "Now let me tell *you* something. Withholding information pertinent to a federal investigation is a crime, Miss Nichols. You could go to jail—and so could Sara."

"But we don't *know* anything," she insisted, her fingers wrapping nervously around the strap of her bag. "We have *not* heard from Jack, we don't know *where* he is—"

"Has anyone else contacted Sara and asked about Jack?"

"Like who?" she asked warily. "What makes you think someone would?"

"I have my reasons, Miss Nichols," he replied shortly and frowned. "Yes or no?"

The memory of the blond man's cold blue eyes tickled a shiver up Aubrey's spine, and she realized how frightened she was at the thought that he might come back. This man is an FBI agent, she told herself, he can protect you. "Yes," she replied, praying silently to Sara to forgive her.

"When?"

"Early this morning. About nine I think. There were two men who said they were with the FBI."

"Could you describe them, please?"

She did, in detail. O'Malley listened without comment. His frown returned, and he sighed as she finished.

"You still have my card?" he asked.

Aubrey nodded.

"Call me if you see them again."

"I will," she promised, then wheeled around and darted for the door.

"Miss Nichols?"

*Oh, not again,* she moaned silently, and turned back to him with one hand on the metal bar. "Yes?"

"Could I give you a ride home?" he asked, his smile returning. "I just happen to be going your way."

"Thank you, no," she replied hastily, pushing on the bar and hoping it was unlocked. It was, and she shoved the heavy glass door open. "I have some shopping to do, but thanks anyway."

Before O'Malley could call her back again, Aubrey fled the theater. Through the rope soles of her espadrilles, the scorching concrete burned her feet. Hot sunlight glared off glass storefronts and the windshields of cars crawling along the busy street. At the corner, Aubrey crossed with dozens of other people, ducking and weaving around them as she made her way quickly to the bus stop. She stood there, fidgeting nervously from one foot to the other, peering through the crowds surrounding her at the front of the theater, now catty-corner across the street from her.

O'Malley didn't come out, and with a grateful sigh she boarded the bus as it pulled up to the curb in a haze of diesel fumes. Her sense of relief was short-lived, however, as she sat down hard on a seat and realized he didn't have to follow her. He knew where to find her.

# Chapter Six

THE bus was packed, stopped every half block or so, and took nearly forty minutes to return Aubrey to the quiet (as quiet as any street in New York could be) block where Sara lived on the Upper West Side. Hot, sticky, and half-sick with worry and fear, Aubrey swung herself around the metal pole in the aisle and down the steps. Still coughing black smoke, the bus pulled away and left her batting at the stench and grit as she trudged wearily toward Sara's building.

On the sidewalk in front of it, his jacket unbuttoned and his cap pushed back on his head, Sam stood smoking a cigarette. He tossed it away when he saw her, reached inside his right pocket, and held out a pale blue envelope.

"Miss Draper left this for you this morning," he said with a half-guilty smile. "She made me promise not to give it to you until at least three o'clock."

It was now nearly four, Aubrey noted, glancing at her Timex as she nodded, took the envelope from him, and turned into the building. She didn't open it until she was leaning against the paneled wall in the elevator. With a cool draft of air-conditioned air billowing down the back of her neck and raising gooseflesh on her shoulders, she tore the flap open and removed the single pale blue sheet inside. The car lifted, but her stomach dropped to her feet as she read Sara's nearly horizontal handwriting:

> Bree, forgive me for ditching you but you know how you are in a crisis, and you know I haven't any choice but to try to find Jack and help him if I can. I think I know where he is and I'll call you—honestly I will—just as soon as I can to let you know that we're both all right. *Don't worry.* You know how *I* am in a crisis. Love you—always—hold down the home front—Sara.

That was it. The end, the limit, the last inch of Aubrey's rope. Hot, tired, worried, and scared to death, she crumpled the letter in her fist as the elevator opened and she burst through the doors.

"Damnit, Sara, you ninny!" She shrieked as she stalked down the hall, jerking her purse off her shoulder and digging inside it for her key. "Of all the numbskull, half-witted things you've ever done, this is *it!* Stand back, world," she cried as she shoved her key in the lock, turned it, and pushed her left hand against the heavy, paneled walnut, "my friend Sara to the res—"

The last syllable stuck in her throat as the heavy door swung open and she gaped at the shambles that had once been Sara's living room. The furniture was slashed, overturned, the wall unit in pieces littering the carpet. Fiberfill from the floor cushions dotted the room like clumps of snow. Dumbstruck yet mesmerized by the ruin,

Aubrey pulled her keys out of the lock, dropped them in her purse, and stepped unconsciously over the threshold, her mouth open, her eyes wide.

She realized then that the door had been *locked.* In that same instant, as every hair on her body prickled, she heard a rattle and a thump—like someone tripping over something—in the bedroom.

"Sara?" a hoarse, whispered voice called. "Sara, is that you?"

Slow, cautious footsteps followed and galvanized Aubrey's panic-frozen limbs. She thought first of running and second of defending herself when she realized she didn't have time to escape without being seen by the person moving stealthily toward the bedroom doorway. Slinging her purse over her shoulder, she bent down and grabbed the first thing her hand closed on—the pink ceramic lamp sans its pleated shade.

As the slow, furtive footfalls drew closer Aubrey cocked the lamp over her shoulder like a baseball bat. Hoping to force whoever it was in the bedroom to reveal himself before he saw her, she moved at a right angle to the doorway. She held her breath to still the rapid hammering of her heart, clenched the lamp with all her might, and waited.

"Sara?" the voice repeated, so low she could barely hear it. "Sara?"

Another thump, this time against the wall, nearly startled the lamp out of her trembling hands. She tightened her grip, drew back her arms, then let out her breath in a startled yelp as Jack, half-crouched, swung around the doorjamb. His arms were extended, his hands clenched around a dull gray revolver. Its snub-nosed barrel pointed straight at Aubrey's throat.

The pink ceramic lamp slid out of her suddenly strengthless fingers and landed with a hollow whump on a half-shredded lavender cushion at her feet. Her head swam, her ears rang, and she probably would have followed the lamp to the floor if Jack hadn't leaped toward her, pocketing the gun and reaching for her in the same swift movement. Strong, but shaking almost as much as Aubrey's mushy knees, his hands closed on her forearms and kept her upright.

For a moment they just stared at each other, Aubrey with her heart sliding back into place between her ribs and her light-headed rush subsiding, and Jack, breathing hard, blinking at her almost as if he didn't recognize her. I haven't lost that much weight, she thought, and tried to decide if the half-bewildered, half-pleased smile just beginning to lift the corners of his mouth thrilled or miffed her.

His grip on her arms relaxed and his thumbs lightly stroked the thin, soft skin on the insides of her elbows. A shiver tickled the base of her spine and her stomach quivered giddily as his smile widened.

"Thank God it's you, Aubrey," he sighed, and shifted his grip on her arms as his dark, almost emerald green eyes slid down the length of her. "At least, I *think* it's you."

Momentarily, Aubrey's knees threatened to give on her again, and probably would have, she thought, if his hands hadn't cupped her elbows then. She'd seen Jack give this same once-over to other women—surreptitiously, of course, when he thought she and Sara weren't looking—but she'd never dreamed that he'd look at her like this. Not once, not *ever,* and for a second or two, as his gaze lifted slowly to her face, she held her breath and savored the wonder of the well-well-look-at-*you* expression in his eyes.

His face, almost boyishly round except for his squarish jaw and chin, looked thinner than she remembered and accented his high cheekbones and straight, thin-bridged nose. It was an exact copy of Sara's nose, straight and flawless, and the unconscious comparison jerked Aubrey rudely out of her giddy, girlish near-swoon as his hands tightened again on her arms.

"Where's Sara?" Jack asked.

"I-I don't know," Aubrey stammered, feeling limp and trembly as his thumbs rubbed the insides of her elbows again. "She isn't with you?"

"No. Sorry I frightened you, Dumpling, but you scared the hell out of me." He smiled and gave her arms a reassuring squeeze. "You okay now?"

Biting her lip, Aubrey nodded. He released her and wheeled away from her, stepping over toppled furniture and split cushions to cross the room and shut the door. Behind him, Aubrey folded her arms and chafed at them with her hands as gooseflesh prickled her skin. She could still feel the imprint of Jack's thumbs and felt certain, as she watched him turn the locks and fasten the chain, that she always would.

"What made you think she'd be with me?" he asked as he turned back to her.

"She left me a letter with the doorman."

While Jack picked his way back to her across the ruined living room Aubrey dug the wadded note out of her purse. She handed it to him as he stopped in front of her, and she bit her lip again as she watched him read it. He looked awful. His thick auburn hair, closely trimmed around his ears, was a rumpled mess. Reddish whiskers smudged his chin and jawline, and his tan corduroy trousers made O'Malley's green tweed suit look like it had just come back from the dry cleaner's. Beneath a lightweight beige poplin jacket, the front of his green-and-brown plaid shirt was dark with sweat.

"Oh, Sara, you little fool," he groaned, closing the letter in his fist as he pivoted away from Aubrey and dragged one hand through his hair. "Why didn't you just wait like I told you?"

"Wait for what?" Aubrey asked and watched his slumped shoulders stiffen.

"Dumpling—" Jack swung around so suddenly she started. "Was she wearing the locket I sent her when she left?"

"I-I don't know," she answered truthfully, her forehead puckering as she tried to remember Sara's outfit. "Her blouse had a mandarin collar and I couldn't tell."

"Damnit," he swore under his breath and ran his hand through his hair again.

He lowered his head, shaking it slightly as he half-closed his eyes. His color was awful, gray and haggard. He looked harried, grim—and *hunted.* Aubrey hadn't any idea why that verb sprang so readily into her mind, but it did and made her shiver.

"You've got to get out of here, Jack," she blurted. "There's an FBI man looking for you and two goons—"

"What?" he interrupted, glancing up at her sharply. "What do you mean, two *goons?*"

"I mean, two big, mean-looking guys who tried to pass themselves off as FBI agents—Sara called them goons."

"How do you know they weren't FBI?"

"Because I told O'Malley about them and he looked about as thrilled as you do."

"Who's O'Malley?"

"The *real* FBI agent. I think he's watching the building too. He offered me a ride home from the theater on the pretext that he just happened to be going my way."

"Oh, Jesus." He shook his head, looked at the floor again, then at Aubrey. "Did he tell you why he's trying to find me?"

"Yes," she said quietly.

"Ah." A slow, bitter smile curved his mouth. "So that's why you're looking at me like that. I expected better from you, Dumpling."

"My name is Aubrey!" she declared vehemently as he turned away from her and started for the bedroom. "And I could say the same about you, Jack Draper!"

"So why don't you?" he taunted, flinging a nasty smirk at her over his shoulder as he disappeared into the bedroom. "I can tell you're just dying to."

Seething, Aubrey followed him, stepping over chunks of the wall unit. She tripped over the leg of the overturned sidetable, saw the photograph of Jack lying beside it, the protective glass shattered, and caught herself on the bedroom doorjamb. On his hands and knees on the floor, Jack was pawing through the strewn contents of Sara's dressing table.

"Innocent men, you know," she told him, "don't run from the FBI."

"They do," he countered as he reared up on his knees and glared at her, "if they can't prove their innocence."

"What are you looking for?"

"Something I sent Sara for safekeeping."

The bell buzzed and Jack leaped to his feet, drawing the gun out of his jacket pocket as he whirled toward her. Her throat went dry at the sight of it.

"Don't answer it," he growled.

They stood staring at each other, Jack's face taut and pale, Aubrey's fingers cold and wet with clammy perspiration, twisting together in front of her. Oh, God, I want to believe him, she thought, her knees beginning to tremble as the buzzer sounded twice more before the knocking started.

"Miss Nichols? Miss Nichols, it's Felix O'Malley."

"Get rid of him," Jack said and cocked the pistol.

Her wavering belief in Jack's innocence shattered with the dull, metallic click of the hammer drawing back. Aubrey started and almost jumped out of her clamdiggers.

*"Go,"* Jack repeated, a threatening edge in his voice.

She went on the double, stumbling her way through the debris scattered around the living room. The bell rang a third long time before she reached the door and croaked nervously, "Y-yes, Mr. O'Malley?"

"I'd like to talk to you, Miss Nichols. I've just spoken to the doorman—"

"Oh, golly, Mr. O'Malley," she called out through the door, her voice warbling unsteadily. "I-I'm standing here dripping wet. I just got out of the shower. Do you—suppose you could come back later?"

"Miss Nichols—" He paused, then asked quietly, "Are you all right?"

"Oh, y-yes," she stammered again, then lied quickly to cover it. "I-I'm freezing, that's all. I've only got a towel on—"

"Oh, I see." He sounded relieved, his voice muffled by the heavy door between them. "Well, I'll wait while you dress."

"But—" Oh, hell, *now* what? she thought frantically. "But I washed my hair too, you see, and I really should dry it—"

"That's all right, I'll wait. I've nothing better to do."

"It'll be a few minutes," she warned.

"Take your time," O'Malley replied. "I'm in no hurry."

Wood creaked as he leaned against the door, and Aubrey shot a now-what? look over her shoulder at Jack. He stood in the bedroom doorway, his back pressed against the jamb, his right arm bent and the gun barrel pointing at the ceiling. He motioned her back to him, and she went, aware of his eyes drifting down the length of her again as she shakily wove a path across the rubble-strewn carpet. As she reached the doorway Jack's left hand gripped her elbow and he towed her behind him across the bedroom.

"Quick." He shoved her into the bathroom. "Turn on the hair dryer."

The bathroom too had been torn apart, and she had to dig through a pile of towels to find the hand-held blow dryer. She plugged it in, stuck it in its wall-mounted holder, switched it on, and nearly screamed as she spun around and saw Jack leaning in the doorway watching her.

His eyes were trailing down her body again, but the soft, well-well wonder in them had vanished. They were hard and cold and made her stomach constrict into a knot of panic as they lifted slowly and settled on her face. Behind her, the hair dryer roared, shooting hot air between her shoulder blades and making her shiver as her hair blew around her face. She tugged it away with shaking fingers.

"Do you have a car?" he asked, his voice low.

"Yes."

"Where is it?"

"Parked on the side street behind the building."

"Can we get to it by the alley?"

"Yes."

"Good." He reached toward her with his left arm, clamped his hand around her right elbow, and drew her out of the bathroom. "Let's go."

Halfway across the bedroom, Aubrey saw the open window, the fire escape beyond it, and realized his meaning. She dug her heels into the carpet, and Jack's hand tightened on her elbow as he spun around to face her.

"What's the matter, Dumpling?" He smiled coldly. "Don't want to run away with me?"

Not like this, she thought but simply said, "No."

His smile twisted, and if the glint in his eyes hadn't been so cruel, Aubrey would've thought that she had hurt his feelings.

"Well, that's too bad," he said icily, "because I can't afford to leave you behind to tell all to the FBI."

"Tell what?" she retorted, trying uselessly to free her arm from his steel-fingered grasp. "I don't know anything."

"Then let's just say it's too dangerous," he replied and jerked her toward the window. "You first," he told her, "and don't forget who's got the gun."

That's not likely, she thought glumly as he let go of her arm and then reached to help her climb through the window. She slapped his hand away from her waist and shot him a warning glare over her shoulder.

"I can manage," she snapped and crawled out onto the wrought iron grate.

They were only three stories up; still Aubrey's head spun dizzily from the height and the heat as she looked down at the brick-paved alley. Swallowing hard, she backed onto the ladder and started down with Jack right above her. She thought first of catching his ankle, then of running as soon as she reached the ground, but both ideas fled from her mind on the second floor grate when she saw the gun firmly clasped in his right hand.

Once her feet touched the sun-baked bricks, she breathed a sigh of relief, then made a face at her dirty, rust-smudged hands. Shoving the pistol and his hand in his right jacket pocket, Jack caught her elbow again and towed her down the dead-end alley toward the street.

"Get your keys out of your purse," he ordered her tersely.

She did and handed them to him, then started and whirled around as she heard a pistol shot and the sound of splintering wood above her. For just a second, Jack's hand loosened on her elbow, then tightened again as he spun around and started running. Every muscle in her body seemed to shriek as his fingers bit into her flesh, jerking and dragging her behind him. Biting her bottom lip between her teeth, she blinked back tears of pain and ran as fast as she could.

"Which way?" Jack panted in her ear as they neared the lip of the alley.

"Left—" she gasped, then nearly screamed as she tripped on the curb and he all but dislocated her shoulder in an effort to pull her up and keep her from falling.

Her red Camaro sat parked at the curb between a yellow Volkswagen Bug and a blue Oldsmobile. Before Aubrey could draw a deep breath, Jack unlocked the passenger door, shoved her into the black leather bucket seat, rounded the nose of the car, and unlocked the driver's door. He slid in behind the wheel, inserted the key in the ignition, started the engine, and jammed the floor-mounted gearshift into first. Tires squealing, the Z-28 shot away from the curb.

Behind them, horns blared and brakes screamed and locked. Covering her head with her arms, Aubrey cowered in her seat and waited for the collision that never came.

"Have a little faith, Dumpling," Jack chuckled

without humor. "I taught you to drive a five-speed, remember?"

Don't think about that, just *don't*, Aubrey told herself and pressed her arms tighter over her head as the ancient memory of her first driving lessons washed over her in a hot wave. He'd taught her the summer before her graduation from Stephens, in the same VW he'd driven down to commencement. It had taken him days, long, patient hours to teach her the finer points of a five-speed transmission, not because she couldn't catch on, but because she'd relished the feel of his hands over hers on the steering wheel and the gearshift. It had been torture, true enough, but the sweetest torture she'd ever known.

And here she was again, stuck in a small, cramped car with Jack, and the old, sweet agony was still there, seeping up slowly from deep inside her. She tried to stop it, tried not to feel the warmth of his body so near to hers, reminded herself that he was running from the FBI and taking her with him, but none of it helped. She wanted to cry, not because she was frightened, but because she wanted him to hold her, to touch her . . .

"Hang on!" Jack said, his voice low and taut.

Lowering her arms, Aubrey looked up at the traffic light just ahead. It was yellow—then red—and she closed her eyes and gripped the armrest on the door. She heard gears grind, brakes squeal, then cracked one eye. A wide chrome grill grinned at her only inches from her window. She leaned her elbow on the door, rubbed her temples, and wondered what her mother would think when she saw her picture on the post office wall.

# Chapter Seven

CERTAIN that at any second Jack was going to pile her brand-new, fire-engine red Z-28 into the back of a bus or worse—and half-hoping that he would—Aubrey kept her eyes closed, her right hand wrapped around the door handle, and her left clenched on the edge of her bucket seat. With brakes squealing and horns blaring around them until her ears rang, she prayed for the wail of a police siren, a flat tire—*anything* that would stop the Camaro and give her a chance to get away from Jack and the memories.

Why, oh why, she moaned silently, is there never a cop around when you need one?—and in the next second she hated herself for wishing it. This is *Jack,* not some criminal, she reminded herself. You know, Jack Draper, the guy you've been nuts about for years?

Then why, argued the part of her that was trying so hard to be logical and sensible, is he *acting* like Public Enemy Number One? If he's innocent, why is he running? Because he can't prove it, replied her other half, the part of her that wanted desperately, because she loved him, to trust him. And you *believe* that?

Oh, Lord, I don't know, Aubrey wailed silently. Look, came the snappy, matter-of-fact reply, if you can't trust Ted Koppel, who can you trust? *Jack,* she argued, that's who. He's never lied to me, *never,* doesn't that mean *anything?* Oh, for God's sake, Bree, her conscience sighed irritably at her in a voice that sounded uncannily like Sara's, don't be such a *hick!*

That thought brought her up short, in the same instant as the Camaro slowed to a sedate speed and she heard a rumbling thrum beneath its tires. Turning her head toward the window, Aubrey warily opened one eye. Steel spans reared high above the roadway, and beneath it a flat blue-gray river shimmered with pewter highlights.

Relieved that they'd managed to get out of Manhattan unscathed and whole, and grateful that Jack was no longer trying to break the world land speed record, Aubrey breathed an inaudible sigh of relief and relaxed in her seat. Almost instantly, her jaw began to ache, and she realized she'd been clenching her teeth. Her left shoulder throbbed and she rubbed at it disconsolately with her right hand as she tried not to look at the man behind the wheel.

"At what time, approximately, did you last see Sara?" Jack asked.

More than she wanted to draw her next breath, she wanted to believe in him, but the creeping suspicion that she was behaving like the naive, gullible person she really was momentarily swung the pendulum of the argument between her heart and her better judgment toward the latter.

"I don't know," she answered, deciding to be obtuse as she kept her eyes fixed on the slate-colored ribbon of water falling behind the Camaro as it coasted down the bridge ramp onto an expressway. "I didn't look at my watch when she left."

For a moment he didn't answer, then said in a flat, hard voice, "I'm not asking you to help me, I'm asking you to help Sara."

"I told you I don't know," she repeated and rubbed harder at her shoulder.

"Are you cold? Shall I turn down the air conditioner?"

"No, I'm not cold," she snapped, and dropped her hand to her lap. "And if you don't mind, I'd rather not talk to you."

He didn't say anything, just made a grumbling noise in his throat.

The throb in her shoulder had eased somewhat, but Aubrey's forearm still ached where his hand had bitten into her flesh. She sighed, leaned her temple against the sun-warmed glass of the side window, and closed her eyes again.

This wasn't at all romantic, not in the sense that the Mary Stewart novels she loved were romantic. Her arm hurt, she was getting a headache, her hands were caked with rusty dirt. The setting wasn't even exotic, just flat, drab stretches of concrete broken occasionally by dusty brick warehouses and marshy, weed-stubbled fields beyond the guardrails that edged the roadway. Everything shimmered in the waves of heat rising from the ground.

Her stomach growled then and she groaned inwardly. Now, to top it all off she was hungry, and she realized that the only thing she'd put in her stomach today was a cup of tea. That explained the headache, but not the empty place in her chest where her heart should be or the tears that smarted just behind her eyes.

While mile after mile of sun-baked highway rolled away beneath the tires, Aubrey held herself as far away from Jack and from any seductive memories as the close confines of the Camaro allowed. She all but sat on the armrest with her temple pressed against the window, but it didn't help much. Her peripheral vision was too good, and every time he moved—to glance in the side or rearview mirror, or to shift his position behind the wheel—her pulse quickened and her insides quivered. She tried closing her eyes, but that was worse. Though she couldn't see him, she could feel him, could hear the sigh of the vinyl seat and the whisper of corduroy against it. How long she sat glued to the door she wasn't sure, but finally her neck felt so stiff it ached and her spine creaked as she straightened in her seat.

"Feel like talking now?" Jack asked.

"No," she replied coolly, keeping her eyes fixed on the glove compartment.

"Look, I'm sorry I had to drag you into this. If there'd been any other way, I wouldn't have."

"I wouldn't have told O'Malley anything. I would've covered for you and given you time to get away." In the corner of her eye she saw him glance toward her, realized that her gullibility was showing again, and added pointedly, "For Sara's sake."

"If I knew how much of a head start she had," he said as he looked back at the highway, "we might be able to intercept her on the road."

"I've told you twice that I don't *know* what time she left."

"Guess."

"Early," Aubrey replied shortly. "Ten maybe, or ten-thirty."

"Damn," Jack spat irritably and glanced at the dashboard clock. "That means she's probably already at the farm."

"The farm?" Aubrey echoed and shot him a wide-eyed look. "Why would she go there?"

"Because that's where I told her to meet me," he answered, turning his head to look her square in the face.

The hard gleam in his green eyes made Aubrey's heart leap in her throat. Hastily, she shifted away from him and locked her gaze on the dashboard. "What's Sara got to do with this, anyway?"

"I told you—she has something that belongs to me."

"The locket? Is that what you tore her apartment to shreds looking for?"

"I didn't ransack the place. Somebody must have come in the same way I did—from the fire escape. It was like that when I got there."

Sure it was, and I'm Twiggy, she thought, her heartbeat still pulsing in her ears as she remembered following Jack into the bedroom and watching him paw through Sara's costume jewelry.

"Those two goons who showed up this morning—describe them."

It wasn't a request, it was a command that gave the pendulum swinging inside her a good hard shove toward better judgment. "Why should I?" she retorted and shot him a sideways glare.

"Be-cause," Jack said slowly, his jaw tightening as he shifted his grip to the top of the steering wheel, "I asked you to help me help Sara."

Now *that's* Jack talking, she told herself. Still, the pendulum had swung too far and she couldn't budge it. "Well, she knows what they look like," Aubrey replied sullenly and turned back to the window.

"One's blond with very pale blue eyes, right?" Jack asked. "His partner's very dark, his hair is cut short, they're both tall, about six-three—"

"How do *you* know?" Aubrey demanded and whirled sideways in her seat.

"I didn't. Not positively, anyway"—he threw her a thick frown, then shifted his gaze back to the road—"until now."

There was something very familiar about the grim look on his face, and though it took her a moment, Aubrey finally recalled that O'Malley's expression had also taken a similar nosedive when she'd described the two men to him. But that didn't make any sense unless—

"Wait a minute," she breathed, wide-eyed. "You *know* them, don't you? And so does O'Malley!"

"I can't speak for the FBI," Jack replied tersely.

"How about speaking for yourself?"

"Don't ask me any questions," he ordered with a sharp, midair chop of his right hand as he lowered it to the gearshift. "The less you know the better."

"Oh, really?" she jeered at him. "I don't know *anything,* and so far today I've been interviewed by thugs and the FBI, and kidnapped!"

*"Please,* Aubrey," he snapped impatiently, "just be quiet."

She ignored him and demanded hotly, "Did you tell Sara the same thing? Did you tell her that the less she knew the better?"

"I gave Sara very explicit instructions, which she chose to ignore," he replied harshly as he shifted into first gear and the Camaro leaped to the left to pass a slow-moving green station wagon in the outside lane. "I'm sorry you got sucked into this—honest to *God,* I'm sorry—but raising hell with me isn't going to change anything. So why don't you just be quiet and let me drive?"

"I can't believe you'd do such a thing," Aubrey continued in a trembling voice. "If you know those two goons, then you must've also known there was a good possibility they'd come to New York looking for you. How could you *do* this? How could you make Sara a cat's-paw?"

"If anybody's a dupe here, it's *you"*—he shot her an angry frown and jabbed an emphatic index finger at her as he lifted his right hand from the gearshift to the steering wheel—"and you can thank my nitwitted sister for that. She's the one who went charging off to the rescue a day ahead of schedule and left you holding the bag."

"She did it for *you!"* Aubrey shrilled at him, her hands balling into fists in her lap. "She'd do anything for you—*anything!"*

"I know that," he said, his voice as tight as his grip on the steering wheel. "And I always thought you would too, Dumpling."

His unexpected use of her nickname disarmed Aubrey and set the pendulum swinging wildly between head and heart. The tears lurking behind her lashes slowly filled her eyes, and his face blurred as she turned away from him.

"So did I," she admitted thickly, "and I still might, you know, if you'd be straight with me, if you'd tell me what's going on."

"What's this? A reprieve?" he asked sarcastically. "You mean you haven't already tried, convicted, and sentenced me?"

"When did I say that?" she challenged, dabbing, she hoped inconspicuously, at her eyes with the back of her hand.

"You said," he quoted, a bitter edge in his voice, "that you expected better of me."

"I said I *could* say that," she corrected him. "I didn't actually—"

"So what's the difference?" he cut her off coldly. "Now if you don't mind, I'd rather not talk to you."

Stung by the repetition of the rebuke she'd given him earlier, Aubrey bit her bottom lip and tried to swallow her tears. Oh, God, she wondered, did it sound that frigid and uncaring when I said it? Probably, she decided, and had to hold her breath to quell a fresh surge of tears. Why is he acting like this? Why is he being so cruel? And better yet, why am I?

Because she didn't have any choice, Aubrey realized, and despite the sun glaring through the side window, an icy shiver laced up her spine. Was it the memories? Or the fact that he'd swept her away with him all right—as she'd always dreamed he would someday—but just to keep her from finking to the FBI, not because he loved her.

It occurred to her then—slowly—that perhaps Jack hadn't any choice either. It made sense, she thought, sort of. Who has time to be Mr. Nice Guy with two goons and the FBI hot on his heels?

Still, it didn't ease the pain of knowing he'd brought her with him for all the wrong reasons. Yes, they were running away—but not together, and when they reached the farm and Sara gave him the locket (she was *sure* that's what he wanted), then what? *Hasta luego, amiga?* Here's looking at you, kid?

What if he and Sara just hopped into her green Mustang convertible and he waved and said, "Thanks for the lift" as they drove off? She'd die, that's what. She'd just shrivel up and die like she'd almost done on graduation day. She couldn't bear it, she just couldn't—

"I'm sorry, Dumpling," Jack said tiredly, his voice, scratchy with strain and fatigue, cutting into her thoughts, "I didn't mean that. I haven't meant half of what I've said to you in the last hour."

Oh, *help,* Aubrey whimpered silently as she squeezed her eyes shut and clenched her fists tighter, don't be nice to me. You're going to do it to me again, you're going to just take off with Sara and leave little pieces of me scattered all over, I just *know* it. . . .

"I'm just not myself, Aubrey, I haven't been since Monday night when all this started. I know that isn't much of an excuse, but I'm just so goddamn tired. . . ." His sentence trailed away in a deep, heavy sigh. "I'll make this up to you, I *swear* I will. Somehow, some way—providing, of course, that I don't end up in jail."

Make it up to me? Fat chance. He could never restore her shattered dream—not *ever*—and she began to wish again for a police siren or a flat tire, anything to save her from the thanks-Dumpling-see-you scene she was convinced lay ahead of her.

It was that bleak, certain fate she foresaw that planted the idea of escape in her mind. Germinating slowly, it sprouted suddenly in a soundless gasp when Jack nosed the Camaro across the lanes of traffic toward an exit ramp. Here's your chance, her brain whispered, to get out while the getting's good, before your heart gets stomped on again. It might work, Aubrey decided, it just might, as a slow, crawling chill shivered up her back and clammy perspiration sprang to her palms.

"I hope you brought money," Jack said as he braked the Z-28 at the top of the ramp. "We're nearly out of gas."

"Yes, I have money," she answered, surprised at how cool and calm her voice sounded.

He turned the Camaro right toward an Amoco station that sat at the bottom of a small hill. While he signaled another right turn into the lot and eased the Z-28 up to the full service island, Aubrey tugged her purse off the floor at her feet and took out her wallet.

"I also have my credit card," she volunteered.

"Cash will be fine." Jack frowned at her as he rolled down his window. "We don't want to leave a trail of charge slips for your friend O'Malley to follow."

She hadn't thought of that when she'd suggested it, but she didn't want to emphasize the point. She handed him a twenty-dollar bill and looped her purse straps over her shoulder as he turned toward the attendant approaching the car and told him to fill it up.

"Do you trust me to go to the ladies' room?" she asked, doing her best to sound snide and sarcastic, once the slim young man in red coveralls had moved toward the pump and inserted the hose in the tank.

Jack nodded, and Aubrey bailed out of the Camaro in a flash. A hot, gasoline-tainted wind lifted her hair off her shoulders as she dashed across the pump lanes and cut around the corner of the white-painted building beneath a sign with an arrow that pointed toward the rest rooms. Halfway to the ladies' room, she heard footsteps behind her, whirled, and saw Jack, his hands in the pockets of his tan cords and the collar of his jacket raised, trailing her up the walk.

"I thought you said you trusted me," she reminded him.

"The men's room happens to be next door," he said and pointed to the sign up ahead.

"Oh," Aubrey said stupidly and ducked through the open door marked "Ladies."

Once she'd shut and locked it behind her, she swung her purse off her shoulder, slammed it against the sink, and tried not to cry. Oh, *damnit,* she cursed, her hands trembling as she unzipped her bag and dug inside for a Kleenex. She hadn't thought he'd follow her. Her eyes blurred, her fingers fumbled through the jumbled contents of her purse—then she caught her breath and her eyes flew to the pale, startled reflection of her face in the soap-flecked mirror as her right hand closed around the canister of Mace her mother had given her.

Her eyes looked huge, her pupils black and luminous. In the hollow of her throat, Aubrey watched her pulse beat as she tightened her clammy fingers around the metal cylinder. Here it was, her chance to dump on Jack before he dumped on her, but she couldn't bear to look at it. Why? Simple. Because she wanted her dream, wanted to be with him, to stay with him. But he didn't want her, not like *that.* Still, she cringed as she pried off the cap with her thumb, touching the trigger with her index finger and closing her fist around the cylinder as she spun toward the door—no, wait, make it look good. She turned back, flushed the toilet, fumbled and lost her grip on the canister, then dug for it again and found it as she inched toward the door.

Still unable to look at the metal cylinder that now felt woefully small in her unsteady grasp, Aubrey withdrew her hand from her purse, tucked her right arm behind her, and looped the straps of her bag over her left shoulder. With her heart thudding in her throat, she leaned against the door and sucked a shaky, shallow breath that tasted like wet paper towels. Oh, God, Sara, forgive me, she prayed, then grasped the knob in her slippery left hand, tripped the lock, and flung the door open.

It banged against the wall like a pistol shot, and Jack, waiting for her, pushed himself off the building as she stepped out onto the walk. He wheeled toward her, one brow cocked curiously, but she shut her eyes, flung out her arm, pressed the trigger—

And nothing happened. She pressed again, as hard as she could—still nothing.

"What is this?" Jack asked, his voice sounding surprisingly mild. "Do you want my autograph or a signed confession?"

Cracking her right eye, Aubrey peered at her outstretched arm—and at the Sheaffer Lifetime fountain pen clenched in her fingers.

"I take it," Jack said simply as his eyebrow slid up another notch, "you thought that was something else."

Nodding miserably, Aubrey bit her lip and sheepishly lowered her arm.

"May I have your purse, please?"

Without comment—what was there to say?—she slid her bag off her shoulder and handed it to him. Fishing inside with his left hand, Jack withdrew the Mace canister and its cap, held them up, and frowned.

"Here"—he held her purse out to her—"you can have this back."

"Thank you," she murmured, looking away from his tight-jawed face as she dropped the pen inside her bag and hooked the strap over her arm.

"I didn't realize you found my company quite so distasteful." He recapped the cylinder with an angry snap and Aubrey jumped. "C'mon, we're blocking traffic."

None too gently, Jack caught her left elbow in his right hand and jerked her back down the walk. Instantly, her still-sore arm began to ache and throb, but Aubrey bit her lip hard between her teeth and stumbled along behind him.

She'd left the passenger door open, and as they approached the Camaro Jack gave her a rough by-the-elbow shove toward it. A sliver of pain shot up her arm, and she all but fell, gasping, into the bucket seat as he strode past her around the nose of the car and swung in behind the wheel.

"Shut the door," he snapped harshly as he slammed his, and the Camaro rocked on its springs.

With tears swimming in her eyes and grimacing in pain, Aubrey awkwardly caught the handle and pulled the door shut. The engine burst to life in a throaty roar and the Camaro shot away from the pumps.

"You didn't have to do that," Jack said, his voice as tight as his jaw as he wheeled the car through a tire-squealing left turn and pointed it toward the highway. "I intended to let you go just as soon as I thought it was safe enough to do so."

That's precisely why I did it, Aubrey thought, but said instead, trying to sound indignant and doing her best to keep her tears out of her voice, "You didn't tell *me* that. It might've been nice if you had."

"Don't bother crying," he retorted coldly. "Tears don't move me."

"That doesn't surprise me," she muttered thickly and rubbed at her throbbing arm.

"And look, goddamnit"—he leaned forward and snapped off the air conditioner—"if you're cold, just *say* so! You don't have to sit over there chafing at your arm like you've got terminal frostbite!"

"I'm not *cold!*" Aubrey shrieked at him. "My arm hurts!"

"What's wrong with it?"

"Nothing," she snapped and swung her head toward the window.

Cursing under his breath, Jack cut the wheel

hard right and the Camaro bounced off the blacktop onto the graveled shoulder. He stretched toward Aubrey with one foot on the clutch, the other on the brake, and his right arm bent on the back of her seat. She drew away from him and huddled against the door.

"What's wrong with your arm?" he asked again.

"Nothing," she repeated, then gasped in the midst of wrapping her right hand protectively around her left elbow as he gripped her wrist and jerked her arm toward him.

"Oh, my God," he breathed, "did I—?"

He left his sentence unfinished and let go of her wrist. Shrugging away from him, Aubrey tucked her hand palm up in her lap, looked down at the black and blue fingerprints on the inside of her elbow, and wished she'd kept quiet.

"I'm sorry, Dumpling," Jack murmured hoarsely. "I hadn't meant to hurt you."

She believed him, or at least she wanted to, and the anguish in his voice only made her feel worse. She didn't say anything because she couldn't; she simply shrugged indifferently and kept her head turned toward the window.

For a moment neither of them spoke or moved. The dashboard clock ticked and the engine thrummed beneath the polished red hood.

"Are you hungry?" Jack asked, his voice sounding tired again.

"Starving," Aubrey replied truthfully.

He leaned toward her then, the seat back sighing beneath his weight, and gently stroked his knuckles through her hair. The light, lush graze of his fingers made Aubrey shiver. Her throat tightened, and self-defensively she pressed herself even closer to the door. His hand caught in midair, and she sensed the tension in the muscles of his arm.

"Please don't touch me," she whispered and held her breath until he shifted away from her and settled himself behind the wheel again.

"Sorry." He nudged the gearshift into first, cut the wheel a hundred and eighty degrees, and made a U-turn back onto the road.

Oh, God, I'm sorry too, Aubrey wailed silently. I'm sorry you never touched me like that before, I'm sorry I grabbed the pen instead of the Mace, I'm sorry, I'm sorry . . .

A half-mile or so beyond the Amoco station rose the golden arches of McDonald's. By the time Jack turned the Camaro into the drive-through lane, ordered two Big Macs, fries and Cokes, Aubrey had mentally browbeaten herself for every mistake she'd ever made. She even apologized—without meeting Jack's gaze, of course—for the twenty-dollar bill she handed him to pay for the hamburgers.

"It's all right, they make change," he replied and kept his eyes fixed on the windshield as he inched the car up to the window. "Keep a tab, will you? I intend to pay you back."

Oh, I'll just bet you do, she told herself bitterly. In spades, I'm sure.

"I'll collect from Sara," she told him flatly, "or maybe there'll be a reward for you."

"I doubt it, I've hardly had time to make the Ten Most Wanted List," he returned shortly. "And I wouldn't be so sure I'd collect if I were you.

Your friend O'Malley could nail you for aiding and abetting a fugitive, you know."

That possibility did more to kill her appetite than the incalculable calories staring her in the face once Jack had lifted the two white paper sacks into the car and handed them to her. Despite the lump in her stomach, she managed to choke down half the sandwich and gladly—but without touching his outstretched hand—gave the rest to Jack, who'd wolfed his down quicker than you could say Big Mac Attack.

The Coke she kept, sipping at it halfheartedly as the sun began to drop lower in the sky and a road sign told her that Ithaca was still a hundred and seventy miles away. Her ever-faithful Timex read five-eighteen, and Aubrey estimated that they'd arrive at the farm somewhere between eight-thirty and nine o'clock. She had approximately three and a half hours to prepare herself for another kick in the ego.

It would be dark by then. How appropriate, she thought, then shivered, and wondered what Sara was doing right now.

# Chapter Eight

RIGHT on schedule, at eight thirty-three according to Aubrey's Timex, the Camaro passed an Ithaca, New York, city limits sign on a two-lane stretch of state highway. Dusk was fading rapidly into night, but Jack, instead of heading straight for the turn-off to the Draper farm, wheeled the Z-28 into a self-service gas station.

"What are you doing?" Aubrey asked, staring at him incredulously as he eased the Camaro up to the pumps. "Sara's waiting."

"She's been waiting all afternoon, what's another ten minutes?" He looked at her askance over his shoulder as he unbuckled his seat belt and opened the car door. "We need gas, and once I've got the loc—" He caught and corrected himself almost instantly. "—my property back, I don't want anything slowing us up."

"Slowing us up on our way to where?" Aubrey asked as she handed him another twenty.

"That," he replied, smiling as he swung out of the car and tucked the bill in his jacket pocket, "is a surprise."

Right up there with blind dates, practical jokes, and singing telegrams, Aubrey hated surprises.

They were always infinitely worse than anticipated. The only surprise she could envision under the present circumstances smacked of late-night rendezvous with trench-coated couriers or submarines lurking off the coast outside the twelve-mile limit. She had never been a devotée of film noir, and both possibilities sent cold chills through her.

To chase away her shivers, Aubrey rolled down the window and let the still warm-and-sticky twilight into the car. On the horizon, the blistering sun that had dogged their day-long flight had nearly disappeared behind a soaring bank of dark clouds. Tall, dusty-leaved trees growing on the fringe of the paved lot whispered restlessly in a sluggish breeze that smelled faintly of rain. Cicadas rasped and insects swarmed around the pole-mounted lights illuminating the service lot.

Glancing in the rearview mirror, Aubrey saw Jack extract the hose from the tank and drag it back to the pump. For the umpteenth time, she wondered how he could stand his jacket in the heat. As he walked toward the cashier's booth, she bent her right arm on the door, leaned her chin on her elbow, and wished it would rain as she watched the kamikaze loop-de-loop of the june bugs and moths around the fluorescent lights of a hamburger stand next door.

When she saw a dark blue sedan pull off the highway and stop beneath the menu painted on the aluminum marquee, Aubrey thought first of screaming and second of fainting. With her brain stuck on overload between the two options, she couldn't do anything but stare wide-eyed at the car as gooseflesh crawled up her arms and she remembered the dark blue sedan that had followed

Sara up the block that morning. She couldn't see who was inside, and no one got out. The car simply sat there with its motor running and its headlights pointed toward the gas station.

In that same instant, Jack slid inside the Camaro, and both front doors on the sedan flew open. Springing sideways in her seat with her heart shooting up her throat, Aubrey clutched Jack's right sleeve.

"It's them," she gasped, flinging a frantic look at the dark blue car. "It's—"

A woman in khaki shorts and a little blond-haired boy in blue jeans got out of the sedan, shut the doors, and walked across the parking lot. Aubrey groaned.

"It's them *who?*" Jack asked, one eyebrow arched curiously as he looked down at her fingers clinging to his jacket.

"It's—well, nobody actually," she admitted sheepishly, and unclenched her fingers from Jack's sleeve. "I thought it was the same car those two men—the two goons—were driving this morning, but I was wrong."

"What car?"

"That blue car over there." Aubrey nodded toward the hamburger stand.

"Dumpling." Jack's eyebrow slid up another notch as he leaned forward and started the engine. "There must be thousands of dark blue sedans in the state of New York."

No doubt about it. The tone of his voice was definitely patronizing, and so was the smile lifting the corners of his mouth. A slow, hot flush crept up Aubrey's neck. She tried to summon outrage but couldn't even muster indignation. The best she could do was a sheepish, lame embarrassment.

"Well, it *looked* like the same car," she said, trying her best not to sound defensive.

"The odds against that are astronomical."

"But what if it *had* been?" she persisted, still trying to make a case for herself that didn't sound foolish and flighty. "And don't quote physics to me."

"I'm not quoting physics." Jack turned on the headlights, put the Camaro in gear, and eased it away from the pumps. "I'm quoting from the laws of probability, which are ruled by chance and governed by luck. It couldn't possibly be the same men in the same car unless they followed Sara."

"I *know* that, I'm not stupid," Aubrey retorted, her patience at his patronizing attitude wearing thin. "It has, however, been rather a rough day, and I'm not used to being rousted out of bed by phony FBI men, lying to a real one, and having the wits scared out of me just because I think I see a man who looks like that blond-haired goon follow Sara up to the corner—"

Still turned sideways in her seat, she barely had time to fling out her right arm and brace herself on the dash as Jack hit the clutch with his left foot, the brake with his right, skidding the Camaro to a squealing halt. Her stomach plummeted to the soles of her feet, not from the sudden stop, but from the thunderstruck expression on his face.

"*Was* it the same man?" he asked, his left hand clenching the wheel and his right the gearshift.

"I don't *know,*" Aubrey repeated testily. "I only saw his back, and then a blue car—"

"A dark blue sedan?" Jack interrupted, his jaw tightening.

"Yes, a dark blue sedan," she replied irritably. "It went up the block behind her and turned right—"

"Jesus, Dumpling!" Jack hit the clutch, first gear, and the accelerator all in one swift motion. "Why the hell didn't you *tell* me?"

The Camaro leaped forward and on two wheels careened out of the gas station. Aubrey gripped the armrest and the edge of her seat, and winced as the Z-28 fishtailed onto the road.

"Tell you *what?*" she demanded, once the Camaro had righted itself and she felt safe enough to loosen her grip on the door and the seat. "And why should I tell *you* anything? You haven't told me a damn thing but to be quiet and let you drive."

"That's a good idea," Jack replied tersely, his eyes fixed on the road as he worked the clutch and the gearshift, springing the Camaro into third gear. "Why don't you just do that?"

The harsh slap of his voice hurt her more deeply than the hot wind that lashed her thick hair across her eyes. Blinking back sudden, needlelike tears, she cranked up her window and pushed her long auburn tresses out of her face.

"Why don't you slow down?" she shot back. "Do you *want* to get a speeding ticket?"

He ignored her and downshifted, and the Camaro leaped through fourth gear and into fifth as it rocketed up the highway toward the turnoff to the Draper farm. The speedometer pushed past sixty, and Aubrey bit her bottom lip between her teeth.

The unexpected response of her sleek little red car to Jack's touch frightened her almost as much as did the other crazy events in this long, hair-raising day. As the Camaro shot down the highway she vaguely recalled something the salesman had told her about the "two hundred and seventy-five horses" in its three-hundred-and-fifty-cubic-inch engine. Now, as the Z-28 bore down on the four-way stop marking the county road turnoff to the Draper farm, she wished she'd paid more attention to the engine specifications than to the color and the thrill she'd felt when she'd realized she was finally slim enough to fit behind the wheel of a sports car without the aid of a shoehorn.

"I know what you're thinking and why," she told him, trying to sound firm, not frightened, "but at that particular corner the only way you can turn is right."

"You haven't the faintest idea what I'm thinking," he answered bluntly, downshifting into fourth and cutting the steering wheel hard left, "because you don't know those two like I do."

*"Who are they?"* Aubrey shrieked at him, closing her eyes and clutching the door handle with both hands as the Camaro screamed through a turn worthy of a movie stunt driver.

Again the back end of the car swerved and slid, then settled down as the tires found a purchase. With her heart in her mouth, Aubrey cracked one eye at Jack. He didn't answer her, and the only indication he gave that he'd even heard her was a not-so-subtle tightening of the muscles in his jaw. She didn't repeat her question, just kept her death grip on the handle and prayed for a state trooper.

Within seconds, the engine backfired slightly and abruptly throttled down. Hoping to see the glow of flashing red lights in the rearview mirror, Aubrey opened her eyes, only to see Jack lean forward and extinguish the headlights.

"What the—"

"Quiet," he ordered. "I'm looking for something."

With only the yellow fog lamps to guide him, Jack leaned toward Aubrey and scanned the right-hand edge of the road as he crawled the Camaro down the curving, tree-grown lane. Alarmingly close to hers, his face gleamed taut and hard in the greenish reflected glow of the dash lights. His shoulder brushed her bare upper arm beneath the sleeve of her sweater, and she hastily pulled herself away from him and the flood of memories stirred by the brief contact. This was hardly the time to remember the countless times he'd touched her, accidentally or otherwise, and certainly not the place to react with a giddy rush of gooseflesh.

"Does your arm still hurt?" he asked and leaned closer.

"No," she answered, and all but flattened herself against the door as a narrow set of weed-grown tire tracks appeared in the amber glow of the running lights.

"Ah, there it is."

Leaning even closer to her, Jack turned the Camaro onto the path and shifted into first gear. The low-slung Z-28 bounced over ruts and humps of grass that scraped the undercarriage. Oh, the muffler, Aubrey moaned silently, as the tall hardwoods flanking the lane engulfed the Camaro and screened it from view of the road. In the faint light of the fog lamps, all Aubrey could see beyond the thin tracks of beaten earth were soaring tree trunks and a wire fence sagging under the weight of thick, woody vines.

"This used to be my favorite place to bring a girl to park," Jack said, his voice low and so near to her left ear that it laced a shiver down her spine.

The tone of his voice was almost offhand and anything but seductive, yet Aubrey's right hand flew protectively to the scoop neck of her sweater. If he saw the half-nervous, half-hopeful gesture, Jack gave no indication. He simply leaned across her, his shoulder so close to her breast that her heart constricted in her throat, and opened the glove compartment. He withdrew the flashlight he'd located there earlier, shut the box, and opened his door as he straightened behind the wheel and shut off the engine and the lights.

"Don't worry, Dumpling," he said, pocketing the keys as he swung out of the car. "I have other things on my mind tonight."

A hot, scalding blush scorched Aubrey's face, and the hand she'd raised to her throat tightened into a fist against her breastbone. A faint rumble of thunder rolled in the distance as Jack leaned back inside the car.

"C'mon, let's go," he prodded her impatiently. "Sara's waiting. Leave your purse—I don't want anything slowing us up."

Shoving her purse as far under the seat as she could, Aubrey opened her door and stepped outside. "Why are you leaving the car here?" she asked, pushing her door shut with her hip and wading through ankle-high grass as she rounded the nose of the Camaro to meet Jack.

"Just in case," he answered simply as he caught her left wrist lightly in his right hand.

"Just in case *what?*"

"Don't ask silly questions," he told her and tugged her gently behind him toward the vine-grown fence.

Cowed, not by the command in his voice, but by the swarm of mosquitoes that attacked her bare calves and arms, Aubrey swatted and slapped at them and envied Jack his jacket and corduroy trousers as he hurried her along the lane and through a break in the tangle of honeysuckle weighing down the fence. She couldn't see the vines in the inky blackness beneath the trees, but she could smell them, the cloying scent almost nauseating in the humid, heavy night air.

Though Jack obviously knew exactly where he was going and wove a quick, sure path through the shadowless trees beyond the fence, Aubrey stumbled occasionally and wished he'd turn on the flashlight he was carrying in his left hand. She wondered why he didn't and almost asked, then decided it would probably be perceived as another silly question. So she kept quiet and did her best not to trip over a protruding root or a fallen branch as Jack led her swiftly through the woods.

Once the trees began to thin out so did the mosquitoes. To keep her hands off the burning, itching welts that she ached to scratch, Aubrey fixed her mind on the comforting mental picture of the Tudor farmhouse, a lamp glowing warmly in the kitchen window, and Sara, framed in its soft light, waving at them gaily from the doorway.

And then . . . and then, Aubrey thought, he'll let me go and leave forever. Her heart quailed in her chest and her fingers wrapped reflexively around his. She thought his grip tightened in return, but she wasn't sure and tried not to think about it. Instead, because she was certain she'd never see him again, she concentrated on memorizing everything that she could about him. The texture of his skin, the shape of his fingernails, square-cut jaw and smooth—

Wait a minute—he'd said he hadn't wanted anything slowing "us" up, and it struck her then, as she began to breath harder and her legs wavered heavily with the effort of keeping pace with Jack's longer strides, that he hadn't specified just who he meant by "us." The two of them? The three of them? Or just him and Sara? Dear God, could he really have meant the three of them? Her heart began to beat faster, and the thought that he might take her with him sent a confused shiver through her spine. Was it panic or delight? Whichever, it was almost enough to make her wish that Sara wouldn't be there.

Instead, to take her mind off her aching lungs and rubbery legs, she let the wind have its way with her hair and punished herself for thinking selfish thoughts by scratching a swollen bite on the inside of her left elbow. It felt so good it hurt, but just as she raised her hand to another welt on the side of her neck, Jack pulled her to a halt beside him and let go of her wrist.

Sweeping the snarled blind of hair out of her face, Aubrey saw that they'd stopped about fifteen yards shy of the juncture of the lane and the drive that ran past the two-and-a-half-story house toward the garage and barn behind it. No one inside could see them from here, but her heart sank as she realized that there were no lights burning in the ivy-covered stucco and timber house. Only the outside security lights were lit, probably, she thought, controlled by a timer during Mr. and Mrs. Draper's absence.

"Where's Sara?" she whispered to Jack, her hands still plastered to her temples to keep her hair out of her eyes. "I don't see her car."

"I told her to meet me in the barn," he replied, catching her hand and tugging her after him. "She probably pulled her car in there too."

"You hope," Aubrey muttered under her breath as she raked her hair out of her face again with her right hand and followed Jack off the now unfenced track.

Why the devil, she wondered as he led her swiftly through the trees, had he told Sara to meet him in the barn? That hardly smacked of innocence, she thought; on the contrary, it smelled to high heaven of a clandestine rendezvous.

Aubrey clung to Jack's wrist as he drew her past the barn. Behind it and just beyond the megawatt wash of the security lights, he broke out of the trees and into a jog. Here the grass had been recently mowed and smelled rich and sweet. She had no trouble keeping up with him as they ran across the open field to the backside of the barn. The door was slightly ajar.

"Take my hand," Jack said as he switched on the flashlight and led her cautiously into the dark barn.

Hay dust and dirt swirled at their feet on the planked floor, and Aubrey cupped her palm over her mouth, a sneeze tickling her nose. Peering around Jack's right arm, she realized they didn't need the flashlight to see that the barn was empty. Her heart began to pound in her ears as Jack drew her forward, calling Sara's name in a low, hoarse voice.

No one answered. There were only a few telltale skitters of mice (at least Aubrey hoped they were mice) in the squarish shadows of feed bins and workbenches beyond the reach of the flashlight beam. Twice more Jack called his sister and swung the light toward the loft. The only reply was a low growl from one of the barn cats. With his fingers tightening on her wrist, Jack backed Aubrey out of the barn and gave her the flashlight while he relocked the doors.

"Maybe she's in the house?" Aubrey whispered hopefully. "Asleep?"

Raking his wind-tousled hair out of his eyes with one hand, Jack took the flashlight from her, grabbed her hand, and led her to the corner of the barn. He stepped out into the open, switched off the light, and frowned at his parents' home.

"I suppose it's possible," he admitted with an irritable sigh. "She hasn't done anything else that she's supposed to, so we might as well look and make sure."

As they passed the garage Jack let go of her hand long enough to turn on the flashlight and shine it in the window. Though she didn't expect to see anything, Aubrey looked with him, feeling a slow, icy chill creep up her back when she saw Sara's avocado green Mustang convertible.

"Oh, my God, Jack," she breathed. "Where is—"

The rest of her question died in her throat as Jack grabbed her wrist and broke for the house at a dead run. Clenching her teeth to keep from biting her tongue, Aubrey pelted across the paved drive behind him.

Outside the kitchen door he skidded to a halt on the flagstone walk and aimed the flashlight at the top corner of the molding. At first, Aubrey couldn't see anything, then noticed the fine, wrapped wires that were connected to the household alarm system running down the wood as Jack lowered the beam toward the threshold. Near the bottom the wires were cut, and she moaned softly in her throat.

Sara had a key—she wouldn't have cut the wires.

Shoving the flashlight at Aubrey, Jack dug in his pocket for his key ring, unlocked the Dutch door, and shouldered it open.

"Sa-ra!" he bellowed, flipping on the wall switch as he leaped into the kitchen and stopped cold in his tracks.

A half-step behind Jack, Aubrey bumped into him and caught her breath, her eyes wide and her knees suddenly weak. The room was a shambles, the cabinets and their contents torn open and strewn everywhere, broken china and glassware from the hutch in the corner littering the overturned tables and chairs.

"Just like Sara's apartment," she gasped, her voice trembling.

Swearing under his breath, Jack grabbed her elbow and dragged her, half-running and half-stumbling, from room to ruined room, as he turned on the lights and searched the house for Sara. The upstairs bedrooms had also been torn to shreds, but Sara wasn't in any of them. His face pale, and his hand unsteady around hers, Jack towed Aubrey down the stairs again and back to the kitchen, where he opened the basement door and tripped the light switch.

Gripping his upper arm in her right hand because she couldn't reach the banister, she stumbled down the steps behind him, nearly fainting when they turned the corner on the landing and she saw Sara lying faceup on the cement floor.

Both her arms were spread palm-up and her knees were slightly bent. Her purse and its contents were scattered around her, her lips were parted, and her head was turned to one side. For all the world she looked like she was asleep—or dead. Frozen on the step above Jack, Aubrey felt the blood drain from her face, and thought afterward that she probably would have fainted if Jack hadn't yanked her arm and pulled her down the steps to Sara's side.

"Pick that stuff up," he said, releasing her hand as he dropped to his knees beside his sister and firmly pressed the first two fingers of his right hand to the side of her throat.

Scurrying on all fours to gather up Sara's possessions, Aubrey heard him sigh heavily behind her, "She's alive," and bit back grateful tears. Oh, God, this is all my fault, she wailed silently, her vision blurring as she crawled toward a tool bench built into the wall to collect Sara's makeup case. Snatching it up, she quickly got to her feet, fumbling with the oversized bag and its copious contents. As she pivoted toward Jack, who'd just risen with Sara in his arms, she kicked a plastic trash can tucked beneath the bench with her left foot.

It toppled over, and the sob swelling in Aubrey's throat shriveled and died there as she watched a syringe and a vial roll out onto the concrete floor. Her eyes flew to Jack's face, but his gaze was riveted to the needle and the bottle.

"Bring them," he ordered curtly and wheeled toward the stairs with Sara.

Dropping hastily to her heels, Aubrey started to reach for the syringe and vial, then snatched back her hand. Stop being stupid, she told herself, there might be fingerprints. Hastily, she dug through Sara's jumbled purse for a Kleenex, found one, wrapped it around her hand, and then carefully lifted the needle and bottle. Holding them away from her at arm's length, she raced as fast as she dared up the steps behind Jack.

When Aubrey reached the kitchen, Jack wasn't there. It startled her so that she nearly wet her clamdiggers. A second later, she heard his footsteps on the hardwood dining room floor and charged after him.

Stop reacting and think, she reprimanded herself, it's why God gave you a brain. Dodging broken chairs and overturned lamps, she followed Jack into the living room, where he was just easing Sara onto the cushionless sofa.

"H-here," she panted, winded and breathless as her quivering knees involuntarily folded her onto the floor beside him. She held the tissue-wrapped syringe and vial out to him.

"Hang on to them a minute and keep quiet," he

said, leaning over Sara as he picked up her wrist in his right hand and bent his left wrist to look at the face of his watch.

The last thing Aubrey wanted to hang on to was the vial and syringe, but she swallowed hard and followed orders while Jack took his sister's pulse. Breathing deeply to catch her breath, she gazed at Sara's face and felt a prickle of alarm on the back of her neck as she noticed the blue tinge to her lips.

"Christ, she has almost no pulse."

His voice ragged with either rage or tears, Aubrey wasn't sure which, Jack laid Sara's wrist on her abdomen and gently lifted her left eyelid. Her vivid blue iris looked dull and her pupil was dilated.

"Gimme that."

Unmindful of the care she'd taken to protect any fingerprints that might be on the syringe or the vial, Jack snatched the Kleenex out of Aubrey's hand and unrolled it on his left palm. With his right he held the vial toward the only righted lamp in the room and uttered the foulest word she'd ever heard him say. She leaned toward him as they both read the words *Sodium Pentothal* on the label.

Only then, once he'd shoved the vial in his jacket pocket, did he lift the opened locket lying in the hollow of Sara's throat. The golden heart trembled as it hung over his left index finger and Aubrey looked at the smiling pictures of Mr. and Mrs. Draper inside the two halves.

"The sonsabitches." His voice shook as he let the locket fall, sliding his arms beneath Sara and gathering her to his chest. "They got it and then did this to her anyway."

*"Who* got *what?"* Aubrey asked, bolting to her feet as Jack lifted Sara and wheeled toward the kitchen.

"The microchip," he answered, grunting a little beneath his sister's weight as he picked his way through shattered furniture.

"What micro—"

"For crissake, Aubrey, later!"

Not the agony in his voice, but the fact that he called her by name, stopped her cold two steps behind him. He'll probably never call me Dumpling again, Aubrey thought, and fought back a fresh swell of tears as she realized that she probably deserved it.

Pushing her own misery away then, she looped the strap of Sara's oversized beige bag over her shoulder and dashed out of the house behind Jack, making sure as she gripped the knob in her hand that the Dutch door was locked before she pulled it shut. Alternating between a trot and a fast walk, he lumbered across the lawn with Sara in his arms, headed for the trees, the tractor lane, and the Camaro.

As she ran to catch up with him, Aubrey saw the flashlight slip out of his left back pocket and plop onto the grass. Bending in midstride, she snatched it up, switched it on, and pushed ahead of Jack to light the path.

Overhead, as they both panted and sweated their way through the woods, the trees whined and tossed in the storm-driven wind. The air was cooler and damp-tasting on Aubrey's tongue with the smell of rain. She glanced up and saw that the stars now were all but obliterated by the clouds she'd seen piled on the horizon at dusk.

In less than half the time it had taken him to tow Aubrey to the house, Jack carried Sara back to the Camaro. Running ahead of him, out of breath and crying at the sight of Sara dangling limp as a rag doll in her brother's arms, Aubrey flung open the driver's side door, shoved the seat out of her way, and scrambled into the backseat.

"Give her to me," she told Jack, holding out her arms to him as he eased his sister's body inside the car.

Sara's skin was so cold that Aubrey nearly cried out as Jack laid her in Aubrey's lap. Please don't die, please, she prayed, smoothing her tousled, matted curls away from her forehead as Jack pushed back the seat, leaped behind the wheel, slammed the door, and started the engine.

It roared to life, the headlights flashed on, and dirt spun beneath the tires as Jack shoved the gearshift into reverse, rocketing the Camaro backward onto the road. He shifted into first, pointed the nose of the Z-28 toward Ithaca, and floored the accelerator. In a haze of burning rubber, the Camaro shot forward, and the transmission whined through second and third gear. The needle on the speedometer, which Aubrey could just barely see through the space between the bucket seats, leaped past forty as the Z-28 lurched into fourth gear and shrieked toward fifth.

"Thank you, Lord, for the horses," she murmured, cradling Sara to her as she herself sagged, weary and trembling, against the seat.

As her eyes drifted shut the glare of headlights rapidly approaching behind the Camaro snapped them open. Easing Sara slightly away from her, Aubrey shifted sideways and winced as she glanced out the rear window at two high, wide-apart beams bearing down on them at an alarming rate of speed.

"Oh, God, Jack," she said, her voice warbling unsteadily, "I think we've got company."

# Chapter Nine

"LET's find out," Jack said, lifting his right hand from the gearshift to adjust the rearview mirror. "If they want a chase, that's what they'll get."

Turning the night/day tab beneath the mirror to *night*, he lowered his hand to the shifter knob and shoved it into fifth gear. As the Camaro leaped forward Aubrey looked over her left shoulder at the rapidly opening gap between their rear bumper and the advancing headlights. She sighed with relief, then felt her heart freeze between her ribs as she watched the headlights close in on the Z-28.

"They're gaining on us," she said, her voice still shaking but not quite as much.

"Damnit," Jack swore. "Belt yourself in, and for God's sake, hang on to Sara."

The whine of the engine jumped up another half-octave, and Aubrey pulled Sara against her as the Camaro roared ahead. With her heart pounding in her ears, she glanced over her shoulder again and saw the headlights still keeping pace with the Z-28.

Every car chase movie she'd ever seen flashed through her mind, and panic coursed through her body with every beat of her heart. According to Hollywood, the good guys never cracked up and always got away. She wasn't exactly sure which side she was on, but fervently hoped, as the Camaro screeched sideways through a sharp left-hand curve, that being an innocent bystander counted for something.

She heard tires squeal and cast another hasty look out the rear window. In the backwash of headlights reflecting off the solid wall of trees lining the road, she made out the boxlike shape of a four-wheel-drive truck as it slid through the curve behind the Z-28. A Chevrolet maybe, a blue and white one, but she wasn't sure.

The license number, she thought, get the license number. Wiggling out from under Sara to get a better look at the wide chrome bumper drawing rapidly nearer as Jack pushed the car at breakneck speed up a low hill, Aubrey squinted in the glare of the high-beam lights behind them and tried to make out the numbers. She was concentrating so intently that Jack's angry shout behind the steering wheel, "I thought I told you to hang on to Sara!" nearly startled her out of her clam-diggers.

"Just shut up and drive!" she shrieked at him as she whirled away from the window. "I'm trying to get the license number!"

"Forget the damn license number!" he shot back, his gaze flicking back and forth between the road and the headlights in the rearview mirror. "Keep your head down!"

Unable to think of a retort, Aubrey stuck her tongue out at Jack's dim reflection in the mirror. Gently, then, she nudged Sara out of her lap, turned backward in the seat on her knees, and flung her left arm over her face to shield her eyes from the bright white glare of the headlights that were now riding practically on top of them.

"*Sit!*" Jack thundered at her, as the Z-28 broke and plunged over the crest of the hill.

Aubrey's stomach plummeted with the car and she lost her balance. Listing to the right, she collided with padded leather side, twisted to avoid falling on Sara, and landed tailbone-first in the seat beside her. Pins and needles shot up her spine and she bit her lip.

"Now *stay* there!" Jack bellowed as he downshifted and cut the steering wheel hard left.

Gears grinding and tires screaming, the Camaro made a perfect one-eighty turn in the middle of the highway. Grabbing at Sara, Aubrey barely had time to pull her into her lap as the Z-28 skidded and then shot down an unpaved side road. Gravel pelted the undercarriage, and the low-slung Camaro bounced over and lurched through ruts so deep that Aubrey expected at any second to hear a tire blow.

With her teeth rattling in her head and her arms aching from holding Sara's dead weight, she looked back over her shoulder. Through the cloud of dirt and dust swirling in their wake, she could just make out the headlights behind them. They'd put a little distance between them and their pursuers, a few yards perhaps, but it didn't last long. The truck, despite the poor visibility, was much better suited to the terrain, and within seconds began to gain ground.

It wouldn't take long, Aubrey figured, for the

truck to overtake them. Didn't Jack know that? Then why in heaven's name—

"Hang on!" he shouted, and Aubrey shifted her gaze to the front of the car.

Her eyes flew open and her breath caught in her throat. A scant sixty or so yards ahead, black letters on a reflective yellow sign nailed to a black and white barricade read "Bridge Out." Horrified, and not at all sure that she or Jack knew what he was doing, she clutched Sara to her and leaned her upper body protectively over her friend. Murmuring a prayer, Aubrey glanced up and caught Jack's eye in the rearview mirror.

"Trust me, Dumpling," he said, but she scarcely heard her nickname as he cranked the wheel hard left and the Camaro spun out in a shrieking circle.

Rock and gravel rained like hail against the windows and fenders as the Z-28 bounced and slid sideways. A loud roar—the truck engine, Aubrey thought dizzily—tore past on the right, rocking the Camaro on its springs. Lifting her face from Sara's hair, she saw Jack fighting the bucking wheel in his hands as the back end of the car fishtailed and swerved with a life of its own. A second later, she winced and recoiled at an ear-splitting crack, then jolted upright in her seat, her eyes wide and staring, as she heard a loud, thudding splash.

The Camaro had come to a stop. Exactly when, Aubrey wasn't sure, but dust was still billowing and drifting across the hood. With his hands lax on the wheel, Jack sat staring into the rearview mirror. He wasn't looking at her, and she swallowed hard, her throat dry and tight, before she turned her head hesitantly over her shoulder.

The whole right half of the barricade was gone and the bent, half-crushed yellow sign swung crazily from the shattered left side. Splintered boards littered the ground, and even though the windows were rolled up, Aubrey could hear the faint slosh and gurgle of water.

"Oh, my God, Jack," she croaked hoarsely, "you killed them."

Slowly, Aubrey turned her head back and looked at him in the rearview mirror. The fingers of his left hand flexed on the wheel as he lowered his right to the gearshift. Both his arms trembled.

"What in hell," he said quietly, his voice surprisingly steady, "do you think they were trying to do to us?"

"That's no excuse!"

Her voice rose hysterically on the last syllable just as a metallic ping whizzed past the car. Until she heard the loud report of the pistol a fraction later, Aubrey thought it was a noise in the engine. When she realized it wasn't, the hair at the nape of her neck prickled.

"They're alive," Jack snapped sourly as he popped the clutch, shifted into first, and launched the Camaro back down the road.

A few more shots rang in their wake, but just as the gravel smoke swirling around the tires had screened the barricade from sight until it was too late, it now made the fast-moving Camaro a poor target. In spite of the gunshots, Aubrey was awfully glad that the men (she assumed they were men) in the truck were alive. She had, she decided, quite enough on her conscience for one day, thank you.

As the Camaro neared the intersection with the highway, she looked down at Sara, her face so deathly pale and still as it rested in her lap. Tears welled behind her eyes, and her fingertips hovered above her mussed and matted curls. Very lightly, Aubrey touched her forehead and wiped away a smudge of dirt with her thumb. Almost imperceptibly, as the Camaro turned off the dirt side road and onto the highway, Sara's eyebrows puckered slightly, her lips moved, and she sighed. Actually, it was more a shallow exhalation of breath than a sigh, but it was the sweetest little exhale Aubrey had ever heard.

"Oh, Jack—!" she cried happily, but he'd already pulled the Camaro onto the shoulder.

In less time than it took Aubrey to wipe the tears dripping off her chin with the back of her hand, Jack had shoved his door open, thrown the seat up, and wedged himself into the backseat on his knees. Lifting Sara's left wrist in his right hand, he looked down at his watch. His lips moved as he counted, then a broad, relieved smile split his face as he tucked Sara's arm next to her and glanced up at Aubrey.

"Her pulse is stronger. Not much, but some."

"Oh, thank you, Lord," she breathed, closing her eyes briefly, then opening them quickly. "What if we get a motel room? Do you suppose she'd be all right if we let her sleep all night?"

"Motel?" Jack echoed incredulously as he backed out of the car and pushed his seat into place. "We're taking her to the hospital."

"Did I miss something?" Her forehead wrinkling with bewilderment, Aubrey watched him slide in behind the wheel and shut his door.

"Like what?" Jack asked as he put the Camaro in gear and steered it back onto the highway.

"Correct me if I'm wrong, but I gather that you need the microchip you put in Sara's locket to prove your innocence, right?"

"Right," he nodded, glancing up at her in the rearview mirror.

"But it isn't there, is it? Whoever drugged Sara took it."

"Right again," he agreed, his gaze returning to the road.

"So how can you risk taking her to a hospital and trying to explain how it is that someone shot her up with Sodium Pentothal? Aren't you afraid that'll look suspicious and that the hospital will call the police?"

"That's a chance I'll have to take," he answered, avoiding her eyes in the mirror as he shifted gears and pushed the accelerator closer to the floor. "Since I'm the one who got you two into this, the very least I can do is see to it that Sara doesn't end up dead because of it."

"I don't suppose," Aubrey said slowly, "that you'd care to tell me exactly what it is that you've gotten us into?"

For a moment their eyes met in the mirror, then Jack looked away.

"What's the point?" He shrugged. "Once I've left you at the hospital with Sara, you'll be out of it."

Just like that—the end of the line. It might be kinder, Aubrey thought, if he would just open the door and push her out of the car.

"And what about you?" she asked, amazed that her voice sounded so calm. "What will you do?"

"I don't know." He leaned his left elbow on the door and raked his fingers through his hair. "I honest to God don't know."

For the remainder of the short, fast drive into Ithaca, Aubrey kept silent and stared out the side window. When Jack turned the Camaro into the hospital driveway, tears blurred her eyes and she couldn't read the name on the marble slab erected in the midst of a grassy, curbed circle. Only then did she glance down at Sara and wonder what she would do. She wouldn't just sit here crying, that was a lead-pipe cinch. Sara would fight, but could *she?*

"Last stop," Jack said as he pushed his door open and got out of the car.

Wiping hastily at her eyes, Aubrey slid her arms beneath Sara and pressed her possessively to her breast as Jack leaned inside the backseat. One eyebrow notched curiously, his mouth opened, but she didn't give him a chance to speak.

"Listen to me," she told him quickly, her voice low and earnest. "Even if I let you take my car, we both know that besides whoever was in that truck, the FBI's looking for you too. We saw your picture on 'Nightline' last night, Jack. How long do you think it's going to take O'Malley to circulate a copy to every police officer in the state of New York?"

A thin smile touched the corners of his mouth as he bent his left elbow on his knee. "He's probably already done it," he answered.

"So how far do you think you're going to get on your own without someone to—"

"Not you," he interrupted curtly and reached again for his sister.

"Why *not* me?" Aubrey demanded, clinging to Sara and refusing to give her up. "Who else have you got?"

Leaning away from her, he parked his elbow on his knee again and turned his head to one side. His hair fell over his forehead, and Aubrey's breath caught in her throat. Oh, God, she moaned silently, *please* don't send me away.

"Why are you doing this?" he asked slowly. "I thought you didn't believe me."

"There you go again," Aubrey complained, "putting words in my mouth—"

"Well, do you or don't you?"

With his elbow still bent on his knee, Jack stared at her, frowning and waiting for an answer.

"I-I want to," Aubrey hedged. "I'm *trying* to—"

"Why?"

"Why what?"

"Why do you want to?"

Aubrey's mouth went dry. "Well, because Sara—"

"—doesn't have anything to do with this," Jack overrode her firmly. "This is you and me, Aubrey—nobody else."

"Well—" she began, her voice trembling, but that was as far as she got.

"Is this why?"

Stretching toward her, Jack slipped his right hand behind her neck, pulled her toward him, and kissed her. Not long or hard or soft or anything else in particular, he just kissed her, then backed away from her.

"I've wanted to do that for a very long time," he said softly and smiled.

"Why didn't you?" she asked tremulously.

"Mostly because—"

Sara moaned in Aubrey's lap then, and they both looked down at her pale face.

"I think we should discuss this later," Jack said, still smiling as he eased Sara into his arms and lifted her out of the car.

Her lips tingling and her legs half-asleep, Aubrey scrambled out of the Camaro behind him, then pushed back the seat and leaned across the steering wheel to retrieve her purse from the floor on the right side.

"Why don't you wait here," she suggested as she looped the leather straps over her shoulder. "I'll go get a wheelchair."

"And leave you to face the questions all by yourself? " One corner of his mouth and one eyebrow quirked dubiously. "I think not."

He hoisted Sara higher, rounded the nose of the car, and hurried toward the emergency entrance. Tracing her lips with the tip of her right index finger, Aubrey scurried after him, still feeling the pressure of his lips on hers. Not hard, not soft, just a nothing-in-particular sort of kiss. Shaking her head clear, she knew this was no time to daydream.

Directly in front of the doors, Jack turned abruptly toward her. "I think you'd better park the car," he said and raised his left elbow. "The keys are in my pocket."

Nodding, Aubrey reached toward his jacket, then flushed as she remembered her aborted escape attempt, and looked up at his face. He was smiling at her.

"Hurry up, Dumpling," he prodded her. "Sara weighs a ton."

Oh, God, he *trusts* me, she wailed silently, blinking back tears as she dipped her fingers in his pocket and pulled out her keys. After all the crummy things I've said to him . . . She bit back her guilty, self-loathing thoughts and threw him a plucky smile. He winked at her, then turned through the door with Sara as Aubrey darted for the car.

Her fingers shaking, she let herself in behind the wheel and started the engine. It purred rather than roared at her touch, and a wryly puckered frown curled one corner of her mouth as she wrapped her hands around the wheel and guided the Camaro away from the curb. The rpm's never once leaped off the gauge, nor did the tires so much as squeak, let alone squeal, as she steered the Z-28 through the lot looking for a parking place. She tried once to pop the clutch and downshift but only managed to kill the engine.

"Sorry, little red car," she muttered, flushing a little as she restarted the motor. "I never knew you had the heart of an Indy racer inside your crankshaft."

Nor had she ever known that Jack could drive like Mario Andretti. Maybe he hadn't known either, she thought, remembering his trembling hands on the steering wheel as she nosed the Camaro into an empty slot between a green Datsun wagon and a yellow Pinto hatchback. Perhaps, she decided as she switched off the headlights and the ignition, he hadn't realized he could until he'd had to.

Thunder rumbled overhead and dull greenish flashes of lightning showed through the cloud-covered night as Aubrey tucked the keys in her purse, slid out of the Camaro, and shut the door behind her. The first, flat, heavy drops of rain splashed and steamed on the cement walk as she ran for the emergency room entrance and pushed open the heavy glass door. The cool air-conditioned air sent a shiver up her back as she hurried down a long linoleum corridor toward a sign that said "Emergency Waiting Area."

The bright light gleaming off the beige walls and tiled floor hurt her eyes, and the smell of antiseptic made her temples ache. Smiling nervously at a uniformed nurse who glanced up at her behind the admitting counter, Aubrey hooked her purse straps over her shoulder, then followed the arrow on the sign to the right and stopped in an open doorway.

The only occupants of the room were a tall, thin young man with brown hair who was pacing the floor, and a plump elderly woman, whose hair matched the lavender flowers in her dress, sitting dull-eyed in one corner. Where's Jack? Aubrey wondered, her heart beginning to pound in her throat as she backed out of the room and glanced left at the treatment area beyond a pair of open double doors.

The drapes were drawn around three of the curtained cubicles. A man groaned behind one, and in another a baby cried fitfully while his mother shushed and cooed. Casting a hasty look over her shoulder, Aubrey saw the nurse bent over an open chart. Slowly, and casually she hoped, she strolled toward the doorway.

Her heart banged so loudly she thought the nurse would surely hear it and stop her, but just as the woman raised her head Aubrey saw a white-coated doctor step out of a curtained cubicle at the far end of the long, wide room. He frowned over his shoulder, raised the chart in his hand and read it, then moved swiftly up the corridor toward the admitting counter. He glanced at the chart again as he walked, looking back at the last cubicle, then shook his head. When he handed the chart to the admitting nurse, he frowned, and Aubrey caught her breath. Doubt and disbelief were stamped all over his long, square-jawed face.

Quickly she ducked out of the corridor and flattened herself against the molding of the waiting room doorway. The baby cried harder, and she bit her lip as she turned her head to listen to the doctor's voice.

"I don't know, Bea," he said slowly, "there's something fishy about the woman in four. Her brother says—"

The baby wailed, so did the mother, and the brown-haired young man nearly sent Aubrey sprawling on her chin as his shoulder collided with hers and he pelted past her. She caught herself on the arm of a chair backed against the wall outside the door, then looked up to watch him run through the double doors a half-step behind the doctor and the nurse. The doctor was the last one through the middle drape on the left and jerked it tightly shut behind him.

The curtain pulled around the last cubicle parted and Jack stepped out. Aubrey sighed, her frantically pounding heart skipping a grateful beat, then settling back into place between her ribs.

Looking up and down the corridor, Jack shoved his hands in his jacket pockets, then walked quickly toward her. Hooking her left thumb around her purse straps, Aubrey rushed to meet him. He reached the doorway before she did, laid his left hand on her shoulder, and turned her around without either of them losing a step.

"Jack, the doctor—"

"I know," he interrupted in a whisper. "Just walk, don't stop, and don't turn around, no matter what."

Though her knees felt suddenly mushy, Aubrey sucked a deep breath and held it as she lengthened her strides to keep pace with Jack. When they reached the exit and he pushed the door open, she sighed with relief and slipped through it ahead of him. Rain pelted steadily against the canopy covering the walkway, and she paused, breathing in the blessedly cooler air, until Jack, as the door fell shut behind him, caught her right elbow in hand and propelled her down the walk.

"How's Sara?" she asked, digging in her purse for her keys.

"Still out of it," he answered, letting go of her arm to unzip and shrug off his jacket.

"Will she be all right?"

"I hope so." Jack sighed worriedly as he draped his jacket around her shoulders and turned up the collar of his shirt as they stepped out from under the canopy.

Their heads bowed against the rain, they ran quickly across the parking lot to the Camaro.

While Jack unlocked the passenger door, Aubrey looked back at the building over the yellow top of the Pinto. A man in a white coat stood at the edge of the walk just under the canopy, his hands cupped around his face to shield his eyes from the rain. The doctor, Aubrey thought, and although he was a good hundred yards away, she could've sworn he was staring right at them. She knew he was, and laid her hand on Jack's arm when the figure wheeled around suddenly a half-second or so later and walked quickly back inside the hospital.

"He saw us," she said shakily and glanced up at Jack's rain-spattered face as he, too, glanced back at the white-coated figure just ducking through the door.

"Get in," he said, frowning as he opened her door and raced around the Camaro.

Oh, Lord, Aubrey groaned as she slid into the bucket seat, here we go again. She tucked her purse under her knees and reached for her seat belt as Jack swung in behind the wheel. He started the engine and moved the gearshift into reverse as he pulled his door shut, and the Camaro rolled backward. It closed with a solid click in the same instant as the buckle on Aubrey's seat belt snapped together across her lap and the headlights flashed on.

"Damnit." Jack spat as he glanced up at the rearview mirror. "Here comes hospital security."

Inching up as far in her seat as the shoulder harness allowed, Aubrey caught just a glimpse of a Jeep with a rotating yellow light on top before Jack rammed the gearshift into first and the Z-28 shot forward, squealing and sliding toward the parking lot exit. Gripping the armrest, Aubrey ducked her chin to look in the right side mirror and watch the Jeep fall behind as the Camaro skidded sideways onto the street and roared off down the rain-slickened street.

A block or so later, Aubrey heard the faint wail of a siren somewhere behind them. A chill shivered up her spine and she caught her bottom lip between her teeth as she glanced at Jack.

"I hear it," he said grimly, his eyes fastened on the road as he shifted gears and the Camaro slid through a right turn.

The tires spun and the rear end swerved dangerously close to a silver Cadillac parked on one side of the residential street, then toward a battered Ford Falcon on the other. Oh, God, *please* don't sideswipe the Cadillac, she prayed, and thought fleetingly of her insurance premiums.

Somehow—Aubrey was never quite sure how, since she squeezed her eyes shut just then and kept them closed until the back end of the Z-28 made a wild swing to the left before straightening out—Jack just managed not to hit either car. When she dared to crack one eye, she saw that they were flying down a narrow asphalt alley overhung with dripping tree limbs and lined with clapboard and brick houses behind picket fences. She couldn't hear the siren anymore, just the squeaky rise and fall of the windshield wipers. Even so, Jack didn't slow down and Aubrey didn't draw a deep breath until they'd left the city proper far behind and the Camaro was tracking rapidly and smoothly down a two-lane stretch of highway.

Despite the soothing hum of the all-weather

tires on the wet pavement, Aubrey's insides quivered, her fingers jumped nervously in her lap, and she found herself thinking *now-what, now-what* in time with the rubbery slap of the windshield wipers. As simplistic a question as it was, it seemed perfectly logical and appropriate.

"Now what?" she asked Jack in a small, tired voice that to her sounded uncannily like a metronome.

"Now to bed," he answered wearily as he leaned his elbow on the door and dragged his fingers through his damp hair.

Though his voice was raw-edged with fatigue, Aubrey started in her bucket seat. Her hands flew first to her throat, and then to the lapels of his jacket, which she hastily pulled together.

"Relax, Dumpling," he assured her with a gentle chuckle. "I haven't slept since Monday night. Ergo, you have nothing to fear from me."

Not at all sure which she was, relieved or disappointed, Aubrey smiled nonetheless and relaxed. "I didn't know that word was contagious," she said as she turned sideways in her seat to look at Jack.

"What word?" He blinked, swiped the back of his left hand across his eyes, and glanced at her.

"Ergo," she said simply.

He looked at her and smiled. "Neither did I," he said softly and reached across the console to squeeze her hand.

A warm, lush shiver, complete with pins and needles that spread across her scalp, prickled slowly up Aubrey's spine as Jack laced his fingers through hers. A wave of heat washed up behind it, and the interior of the car suddenly felt stifling.

Looking down at his hand resting on the top of her thigh, she raised her hand to the window crank and nudged the glass down a discreet inch or two. The rush of cool rain against her cheeks made her breath catch in her throat, and she murmured an inaudible thank-you for the darkness that masked her certainly vermilion face.

Twice, softly, his thumb stroked hers, and Aubrey's heart leaped in her breast, first with surprise, and then with hope. Countless times in the almost twelve years that she'd known Jack he'd held her hand, but he'd never added an intimate little caress. Maybe this is it, she thought—The Moment, The Touch. A thousand times in a thousand different ways she'd fantasized this, but she'd never dreamed . . .

Scarcely breathing, Aubrey closed her eyes and savored the absent half-moons his thumb was tracing across the back of her hand. Clockwise, counterclockwise, clockwise again—then he gently squeezed her hand and released it.

"I wish I hadn't quit smoking," Jack said tiredly. "I could sure use a cigarette."

"So could I," mumbled Aubrey, who'd never smoked in her life, as she bent her right elbow on the armrest and glumly watched the rain-soaked fields and dark farmhouses roll by the right side of the car.

Disappointed, she decided firmly, that's definitely what she was. Disappointed.

In the reflection of the headlights bleeding across the wet pavement, Aubrey saw a sign ahead marking a three-way stop. Jack braked the Camaro, changed gears, and made a right turn at normal speed without any stunt-driver flourishes.

A mile or so down the narrower road, just shy of a one-lane bridge, Jack slowed again and turned the wheel left. The Z-28 bounced gently off the pavement, over the shoulder, and slid out of sight around a curve into a tree-grown lane that was barely wide enough to accommodate the low, sleek car.

Though the rain had slowed now to a drizzle, Aubrey still wondered about mud, but as she stretched forward in her seat and peered over the dashboard, she saw that the ground illuminated by the headlights was beaten grass and weeds. There wasn't a bare patch of dirt in sight, and she sighed with relief as Jack killed the lights and the engine and picked up the flashlight from the console where Aubrey had left it.

"Here, hold this," he said as he passed her the light and dug in his right pants pocket.

He withdrew Sara's locket and glanced at Aubrey. "You wouldn't happen to have a pair of tweezers in your purse, would you?"

"I think so," she said, her eyebrows wrinkling curiously as she handed him the flashlight and tugged her bag out from under her knees. "Why did you take the locket?" she asked as she unzipped her purse in her lap and fished inside for her manicure kit. "I thought you said the chip was gone."

"It probably is," he told her, a rueful smile lifting one corner of his mouth. "Still, it never hurts to check."

"Is it very small?" Aubrey asked as she unzipped the pink leather case and worried a pair of tweezers out of the satin loop that held them.

"Pretty small," he said as he handed her the flashlight again and she gave him the tweezers.

While he opened the locket and carefully lifted his mother's picture Aubrey held the flashlight over his right shoulder. In its white glare, his face, except for the darkish stubble of beard, looked almost as pale as Sara's. Lifting the fingertips of her left hand to her lips, Aubrey smirked ruefully. You dummy, she thought, that tingling when he kissed you wasn't magic, it was whisker burn.

Holding the photo carefully with the tweezers by one heart-shaped corner, Jack turned it over and frowned. "Gone," he sighed, and replaced it.

"You didn't really expect it to be there, did you?"

"No, not really." He sighed again, heavily, as he slouched in his seat and frowned at the open locket hung over his left index finger. "It just strikes me as odd, though, that after they'd lifted the chip, they put the picture back. And if they were going to go to that much trouble—which obviously they did to make it look like the photo hadn't been disturbed—then why didn't they close the locket? Why was it open when we found Sara?"

"That *is* strange," Aubrey murmured thoughtfully, then asked, "Why did they leave her in the basement, Jack?"

"To lessen the odds that someone would find her," he said grimly and pinched the locket shut with his thumb.

The snap made Aubrey jump. Her right arm jerked and the flashlight beam raked across Jack's face.

"Sorry," she mumbled, shivering as she switched

it off and laid it on the console. "They meant to kill her, didn't they?"

"Of course they did." He bent his left elbow on the armrest, raised his hand, and pressed the locket to his chin as he stared at the rain-splattered windshield. "There were two needlemarks in her arm, which means the first injection was just enough to make her talk and tell them where the chip was. . . ."

He didn't add, "And the second one was enough to kill her," but he didn't have to. Gooseflesh crawled up Aubrey's arms. She shivered again, but she knew she wasn't cold.

"The two goons did it, didn't they?" she asked.

"I don't know." He cupped the locket in his palm, bent his head, and rubbed his eyes with his thumb and first finger. "It was either them or a couple other of Lawrence's heavies."

"Lawrence?" Aubrey echoed. "Why does that name sound—" She caught her breath then and looked sharply at Jack, who was just a dim outline in the darkness against the door. "I remember now. Sara and I saw him on 'Nightline' too. The report said he was the last person to be seen with you. Sara tried to call him—"

"She *what?*" Jack bolted upright in his seat.

"She didn't get him," Aubrey went on quickly. "His home phone has been disconnected, and no one answered at his lab."

"You're *sure* she didn't talk to him?" Jack asked, his voice low and earnest as he leaned toward her.

"No, I—at least, I don't *think* so," she answered uncertainly. "We went to bed shortly after that. Unless she woke up before I did—I can't be sure that she didn't, you see, because I slept in the living room. Those two goons leaning on the buzzer woke me, and Sara looked like she'd just gotten up when she came out to answer the door, but I suppose she could've been awake for some time. And then there is an extension in her bedroom."

"Oh, Jesus." Jack exhaled slowly and shifted away from Aubrey. "If Lawrence is in this, too, then we've got big trouble."

"I don't understand why he would be. Sara called him Uncle Hugh, and she said he was an old friend of your parents."

"I thought he was too." Jack made a fist out of his right hand and tapped it against the steering wheel. "That's why I took the chip to him. Now I wish to God I hadn't."

He didn't say anything else, he just sat there tapping his fist absently against the steering wheel and staring at the windshield. What chip? Aubrey wanted to shriek at him, but she didn't. Bit by bit he was explaining, and though she wasn't sure that he was even aware that he was, she had a hunch that if she kept quiet and didn't press him, he'd eventually tell her the whole story.

"I wish to hell I'd taken the time to make another copy." He sighed, leaned forward, and started the engine.

"Oh, no." Aubrey asked sympathetically. "The chip in Sara's locket was the only one?"

"No." He pulled on the headlights, put the gearshift in reverse, and braced his right hand on the headrest of Aubrey's seat as he backed the Camaro out of the lane. The wheels spun just a little on the wet grass. "It was a copy of the one I set fire to in Hugh's lab yesterday."

"*What?*" Managing, just barely, to keep the shriek out of her voice, Aubrey balled her fists in her lap and said between clenched teeth, "Look, Jack, I'm *trying* to be patient, but if you don't tell me what's going on—"

"Calm down, Dumpling, I *am* telling you." He glanced her a brief smile as the Camaro bumped out of the lane, then his expression sobered as he turned the car down the road toward the bridge. "On Monday morning, Jeb Parker—my lab assistant at Nu-Lite—was found dead in his apartment. The police theorized that he'd been shot trying to stop a burglar. I was . . ." He paused, frowned, and dragged his fingers through his hair as he leaned his left elbow on the door. ". . . shocked, naturally, and doubly so when I came home from work Monday night and found a package from Jeb. He'd mailed it to me on Saturday, and inside there were two microchips and a note from Jeb that said he knew he was being watched by Nu-Lite security people and that he was sending the enclosed—copies of a file that he'd accidentally accessed in Nu-Lite's main computer and all our research notes on the LC-15—to me as a precautionary measure. Well, all of a sudden, I began to doubt the burglary theory, and PDQ slipped one of the chips into the locket, which I'd intended to send Sara for her birthday anyway, and express mailed it to her Tuesday morning with a note explaining what was inside, and with instructions to contact the police within forty-eight hours if I suddenly disappeared or something."

"But why," Aubrey asked as Jack paused to

shift gears, "did you make the two-day stipulation?"

"I'd hoped"—he cast her a sour look—"to keep Sara from charging off to save the day and to avoid exactly what we're going through now."

"I think she intended to wait," Aubrey told him, "but those two—the goons—frightened her."

"I'm sure they did," he agreed, wrapping his left hand around the wheel as he rubbed his upper arm beneath his sleeve with his right. "They scared the hell out of me outside Hugh's lab yesterday."

"So that's how you know them," Aubrey said, and when Jack nodded, her throat tightened. "Did you know they'd come after the chip?"

"They weren't after the chip," Jack corrected her emphatically and glanced her a sharp frown. "They were after *me.* Hugh knew damn good and well that if I contacted anybody I'd contact Sara, and I was very careful *not* to leave the package receipt lying around. I destroyed it."

"So they just got lucky?"

"Yes, they just got lucky."

He turned his head and looked at her again, waiting.

"Okay." Aubrey shrugged. "They got lucky."

He smiled a little and glanced back at the road. "The only thing you haven't explained is what was on the chip—besides the LC-15, I mean—and how Lawrence got involved in this."

"The file that Jeb stumbled onto in the computer first of all was unaccessed, which meant it was pure luck that he found it. Second, it was in code, but Jeb knew enough cryptology to tumble right away to the fact that it had something to do with the LC-15. He copied the file, uncoded it, and discovered that John Collins, president of Nu-Lite, has for years been misappropriating funds from government grants to finance his personal pet research projects—"

"Oh, *no*," Aubrey groaned. "Don't tell me the LC-15—"

"Exactly." Jack nodded. "There were certain notations in the file which led Jeb to conclude that Collins was about to blow the country to avoid an upcoming congressional investigation and probable prosecution. That, of course, would have left me, as project head for the LC-15, holding the bag for the missing funds. Of course, I didn't know any of this until Tuesday afternoon after I'd viewed the chip at Hugh's lab."

"So that's how he got into this? But why did you take the chip there?"

"Because when I got to work Tuesday morning —after I'd mailed the second chip to Sara—Collins was in my lab. He demanded the LC-15 research, which he'd already discovered had been pulled out of the computer. He'd settle for my notes, he said, and threatened all kinds of ugly stuff if I didn't hand them over. I agreed, knowing, of course, that Jeb had already transferred them to the chip and then destroyed them." He paused again and gave Aubrey a wry smile. "I really think I deserve an Oscar for my role as outraged scientist when I discovered that some fink had broken into my lab and stolen my notes."

"Did Collins believe you?"

"I thought he did, but around lunchtime I noticed that wherever I went in the building, a Nu-Lite security guy or two or three went too. I told my secretary I was leaving for the day, and a few blocks away from the lab managed to slip the tail Collins had put on me. I called Hugh then, because I thought I could trust him, and took the chip over there to view it. Fool that I am, I let him look over my shoulder. He told me that a project like the LC-15 was just what he needed to pull his lab out of the red. He offered me two hundred and fifty thousand dollars for the chip and guaranteed safe passage out of the country to avoid taking the rap for Collins. I refused, he pulled a gun, and that's when I torched the chip in a petri dish."

He cast Aubrey a sheepish, sideways smile and chafed at his left arm again.

"I don't suppose," she asked gently, "that he just let you go, did he?"

"Oh, hell no. He sicced those two charming gentlemen who visited you and Sara this morning on me. How I managed to get free of them I have no idea, and *please* don't ask. That part of yesterday is but a blessed blur in my mind, and I'd just as soon leave it that way." He stopped rubbing his arm and lowered his right hand to the gearshift. "I tried to go back to my apartment to pick up a few things, but the boys from Nu-Lite were lurking around the pool, so I just headed straight for the airport and hopped a flight for New York. The way my luck had been running, I wasn't at all surprised when the plane developed an engine problem and was forced down in Albuquerque. I had to wait for another flight and tried to call Sara then, but there was no answer." He stifled a yawn and rubbed at his eyes again. "That was about seven o'clock last night, I think."

"We went out for dinner," Aubrey told him quietly.

"While I waited, I had a drink in one of the lounges and saw the phony story Nu-Lite had leaked about me and the unidentified foreign government on the evening news. The FBI was in it by then, and I figured commercial airlines would be the first place they'd start looking for me. So I left, hitchhiked to a private airstrip where no questions were asked as long as you had cold cash, and chartered a plane to New York. The rest you know."

"Yes, the rest I know," she murmured, a troubled frown wrinkling her forehead as she turned sideways in her seat to face him. "You're the cat's-paw, aren't you?"

"I guess I am." He looked at her, smiled thinly, and laid his right hand over her left. "I guess we both are, Dumpling."

# Chapter Ten

"AND Sara too," Aubrey added quietly.

"Yes, Sara too," Jack agreed as he squeezed her hand and then yawned widely.

His shoulders shivered and Aubrey felt a slight tremor in the hand cupped over hers. The steering wheel wobbled a little beneath his left hand and the nose of the Z-28 veered toward the center line.

"Want me to drive?" she asked.

"Might not be a bad idea." He cast her a sideways smile, then stifled another shuddery yawn as he eased the Camaro off the road and onto the shoulder. "We've got to change places before we get to the motel anyway."

"Motel?" Aubrey echoed. "What motel?"

"The one just a mile or so up the road," he answered as he opened his door and motioned her to do the same. "The one you're going to check us into—under a false name, of course."

"But, Jack," she objected as she got out of the car, hurrying around to meet him in front of the headlight beams. "Won't they want to see some ID?"

"This isn't the Hilton, Aubrey." He smiled at her as they crossed paths and he walked around the right side of the car. "They couldn't care less who you are. It'll be no sweat."

"Oh, I don't know," she hedged, a nervous tremor in her voice as she glanced at him over the rain-spattered roof of the Camaro. "What if I say my name is Mary Smith and then they ask to see my license?"

"Don't use such a generic name," he told her, and Aubrey had to slide hurriedly in behind the wheel to hear the rest of what he said. "And in the second place"—he paused to shut his door—"just offer to pay in advance, flash a twenty, and you'll have a key in your hand before you can say Howard Johnson."

"It's not that I don't trust you," Aubrey lied as she steered the Z-28 back on the road, over the crest of a small hill, and saw a flickering red "Vacancy" sign about a quarter of a mile ahead on her left. "But how can you be so sure?"

"I'm sure," he assured her around another yawn, "because I used to frequent this establishment under the name John Reed with certain young female classmates of mine at Cornell."

"Oh, really?" she replied, she hoped offhandedly, as she nosed the Camaro into the motel drive and narrowly missed sideswiping the mailbox on the side of the road. "What a fascinating bit of nostalgia."

Her attempt at being nonchalant fell flat. She knew it even before Jack's chin turned sharply in her direction. It was too late to take it back, however, so she simply lifted her chin, clamped her hands on the wheel, her eyes on the drive, and floored the accelerator.

Spinning gravel, the Camaro rocketed up the

sloping yard. The sudden forward thrust shoved Jack even lower on his spine and flattened him against the back of the bucket seat. Well out of view of the office, Aubrey skidded the Z-28 to a halt, shoved the gearshift into neutral, yanked on the parking brake, snatched up her purse, flung open her door, and stalked toward the office, leaving Jack floundering off-balance on his tailbone.

All in all, she thought, wincing as sharp chunks of gravel bit into the soles of her espadrilles, it was an asinine and bitchy performance—one that had given her a lot of personal satisfaction, however, and that bolstered her flagging confidence as she stepped up on a weather-beaten porch and faced the office of what she thought was certainly a sleazy, X-rated adult motel.

Shaking out some of the fine mist that had caught in her hair, Aubrey drew a deep breath and opened the old-fashioned wooden screen door. As she stepped over the threshold a long-faced man who bore a striking resemblance to Ichabod Crane looked up at her from behind a high polished counter with a rack of bright, cheery postcards in one corner.

"Good evening," she said, smiling at him as her gaze darted nervously from the oak paneling on the walls and the chintz curtains on the windows. "I'd like a room, please."

"Most folks do who stop in," the man replied dryly.

He didn't smile, and though Aubrey wasn't sure if he was making a joke or being snide, she chose to smile even wider as she withdrew her wallet from her bag and pulled out a twenty-dollar bill. She laid it on the faded leather blotter in front of him and wrapped her fingers around her purse straps to keep them from shaking.

"Just for tonight," she said, "and I'd like to pay now, please, because I'll be leaving very early."

"Fine, lady." He half-turned, reached a key off a peg, and slid it across the desk to her as he nodded at the open guest register. "Number seven around back. If I ain't up in the mornin' just drop the key through the mail slot."

"Thank you." Aubrey picked up a blue Bic pen from the desk, wrote the only name she could think of—Mary Smith—and smiled again as she whipped up the key. "Good night."

"G'night, lady." He nodded briefly and picked up the twenty-dollar bill.

No sweat, just as Jack had said it would be. Feeling ridiculous, and hating herself for it, Aubrey pushed through the screen door and let it slap shut behind her. If he says one word, she thought, making a fist around the key in her palm as she hurriedly rounded the building to the Camaro, I think I'll slug him.

"Any problems?" he asked, straightening in his seat when she got in behind the wheel.

"None," Aubrey replied stiffly as she put the car in gear and drove it around the building.

Yellow insect bulbs burned outside the rooms, which were white clapboard cottages with blue doors and shutters. Somehow, Aubrey had thought the lights would be red. Three other cars were parked in the covered ports that connected the cottages, and the Z-28 slid with room to spare into the space reserved for number seven. While Aubrey switched off the lights, the wipers, and the engine and picked up her purse, Jack reached between the seats to retrieve Sara's handbag and his jacket, which Aubrey had removed. He took the key from her as they got out of the car, and she followed him up the neatly weeded flagstone walk.

Checking into a motel with Jack was one thing that Aubrey had never fantasized. All her daydreams of him had revolved around a happily-ever-after ending, and cheap, tawdry motel rooms just didn't seem the right kind of place to kindle a happily-ever-after beginning. Expecting heaven-only-knew-what, she hung back as Jack unlocked the door, switched on the lights, and entered the cottage.

Holding her breath again, Aubrey peered hesitantly around the doorjamb, watched him toss his jacket on the foot of the double bed, and then upend Sara's handbag in the middle. The contents tumbled out onto a beige and blue striped spread that complemented the beige pile carpet and matched the drapes on the two small windows. While Jack pawed through Sara's things Aubrey eased over the threshold and looked, wide-eyed, around the room. The maple furniture, a chest, dresser and small desk, wasn't expensive, neither was it scratched or burned, and it had been freshly polished. A wing chair that matched the bedspread sat in the near corner beside a chrome floor lamp, and the whole cottage smelled, but not unpleasantly, of Lysol.

"Bless you, Sara Heartburn, and your suitcase-sized handbags." Jack, with a package of disposable razors in one hand and a can of Gillette Foamy in the other, turned around and grinned at Aubrey. "Say what we will about my baby sister, she never goes off to save the world unprepared. Take a look . . ." He gestured toward the bed with the can of Foamy as he rounded the foot of the bed toward the bathroom. "I don't think she forgot much, if anything."

As he kicked the door shut behind him Aubrey swung her purse off her shoulder and slid it onto the dresser. So where are the stag movies? she wondered grimly, glancing up at the ceiling as she crossed the room to the bed.

"Disappointed?"

Startled by his half-chuckled question, Aubrey tripped over nothing and quickly lowered her gaze. Leaning on his right shoulder in the now-open doorway, Jack was smiling at her.

"You were expecting a mirror on the ceiling, perhaps?" He folded his arms across his chest and his smile widened. "And a bed that does the rhumba when you feed it quarters?"

Though she really didn't think a lie would wash here, Aubrey tried one anyway.

"Of course not," she replied evenly. "I thought I saw a spider."

Miraculously she managed not to blush, but quickly, just in case her luck didn't hold, she bent her head over the contents of Sara's voluminous beige leather handbag. Besides the makeup case that Aubrey had picked up off the basement floor, Sara had managed to cram deodorant, toothpaste, toothbrushes still in their boxes, a compact, fold-up hair dryer, trial sizes of shampoo and cream rinse, a pink nightie with lace straps, argyle socks, jockey shorts, a Cornell T-shirt, and a pair of Jack's gray jogging shorts that she'd seen on a shelf in Sara's closet the day before, a pair of cuffed khaki shorts, a lavender brassiere and panties, and a madras plaid blouse.

"Since you've obviously been starving yourself for some time, I think Sara's things will fit you," he said mildly, "except maybe her underwear."

The last of her luck ran out, and Aubrey felt her face flame as her chin shot up defiantly. Jack had moved out of the doorway and was leaning against the desk. His smile, however, vanished abruptly.

"I'll wash mine out in the sink, thank you," she said between clenched teeth as she snatched up the nightie, the deodorant, and the shampoo and cream rinse.

"Dumpling—" he began, pushing himself off the desk as she stalked past him.

Eluding the hand he had stretched toward her, Aubrey nipped into the bathroom. She slammed the door behind her, locked it, and *then* realized that she'd taken offense at being teased because she was thin. This was a totally new experience for her, one that sat her down hard on the lowered lid of the toilet with Sara's nightie still clenched in her left hand.

Who, *me?*

Half-turning, she set the toilet articles next to the razors and shaving cream on the top of the flush tank, rose, and stood in front of the mirror. Shaking out the nightie by its lace straps, she cocked her head dubiously to one side and raised it to her shoulders. Despite her wind-snarled hair and runny, smudged mascara, a slow smile spread across her mouth as she realized that, by golly, it looked like it *would* fit.

Of course, there was only one way to make sure.

Hastily she draped the nightie over a towel

rack, drew the shower curtain across the bathtub, turned on the taps, and adjusted the spray. She stripped off her clothes, barely noticing the burrs that had snagged her sweater and the hole in the right knee of her grass-stained clamdiggers, then picked up the shampoo and stepped into the shower.

Once she'd scrubbed her body until her skin hurt, shampooed her hair, and wrapped a towel around her wet head, she turned off the water and hung her facecloth to dry on the shower rod. Drawing the curtain aside with a trembling hand, she quickly toweled off, got out of the tub, and drew Sara's nightie over her head.

It fit—what little of it there was.

Dismayed at how much of her lightly freckled breastbone showed above the lace-piped bodice, Aubrey bit her lip at her reflection and backed across the room on tiptoe to get a better look at her lower half. Oh, Lord, she moaned silently, tugging at the bottom hem. Almost everything showed, including the faint stretch marks on her outer thighs that no amount of Vitamin E cream could or probably ever would eradicate.

How on earth, she wondered, as she gave up trying to rearrange the scanty gown to cover certain strategic areas of her anatomy, was she going to navigate around a motel room with Jack, practically in her altogether? She couldn't put her filthy, all-but-ruined clothes back on. That would make her look prudish and naive (which of course she was), so instead she draped one towel around her shoulders, knotted another around her waist, scooped up her clothes, and threw the door open before she lost her nerve and decided to sleep in the bathtub.

Stretched out half-asleep on the bed, Jack started and his eyes flew open at the sound of the door opening. Ducking her head and clutching the towel around her shoulders, Aubrey scurried past him, dumped her clothes and shoes in a pile on the floor and curled up in the wing chair in the corner.

"The bathroom's all yours," she told him as she snatched up a three-month-old copy of *Reader's Digest* from the nightstand, yanked it open, and buried her nose in it.

Over the top of the magazine, with her heart pounding in the hollow of her throat, Aubrey watched him sit up, swing his legs over the side of the bed, and look at her over his shoulder. Because his rumpled hair had drooped over his forehead she couldn't be sure, but she thought he was smiling.

"Isn't it rather difficult to read upside down?" he asked.

She blinked to focus her eyes, saw that the magazine was, in fact, wrongside up, and latched onto the first plausible-sounding lie that popped into her frantically overworked brain. With what she hoped was a haughty lift of her head, she lowered the *Digest* and looked down her nose at him.

"I am reading the key to a personality quiz," she informed him coolly.

"I beg your pardon." His smile quirking to one side, Jack pressed a hand to his chest and pushed himself to his feet. "I thought perhaps you were having an anxiety attack at the idea of being alone with a man in a motel room."

"I don't have anxiety attacks anymore." Aubrey pressed the open magazine to her throat to cover the telltale flush spreading up her breastbone. "It was my last year's New Year resolution."

"That's splendid," he said, undoing the first two buttons of his shirt as he walked around the bed and sat down on the side closest to Aubrey. "I'm glad I'm not making you nervous."

"Well, of course you're not," she assured him and pressed the magazine tighter to her chest.

"That's good," he said as he picked up Sara's makeup case, unzipped it, and dug inside until he found the small plastic bottle of hydrogen peroxide she kept to medicate her perpetually infected pierced ears, "because I'm too tired to sleep on the floor."

"I beg your pardon?" Aubrey asked warily.

"I said I'm too tired to sleep on the floor." Jack put the case aside, stuck his hand in his left jacket pocket, and withdrew a small roll of gauze.

"Maybe I'm thickheaded," she began, "but I don't see—"

"It means," Jack said, smiling at her over his shoulder as he walked into the bathroom, "that we'll be sharing the bed."

"That's what *you* think," Aubrey muttered, frowning and wondering what in the world he was going to do with gauze and hydrogen peroxide as he closed the door between them.

More times than she could count, Aubrey had told Sara that her ears would clear up if she'd just stop buying ninety-nine-cent earrings and invest in a good pair of fourteen-carat gold. She'd never listened though; she had a penchant for flashy, dime-store earrings. Aubrey's eyes puddled as she thought of Sara lying comatose and alone in the hospital.

To take her mind off Sara, Aubrey closed the *Digest,* laid it on the nightstand, and left the chair for the bed. As she listened to the muted rush of the shower in the bathroom she unfolded Sara's dryer and carried it to the dresser, where she retrieved her brush from her purse. Her head spun a little as she dropped to the floor to plug in the dryer, and her stomach growled. Pulling herself up by the dresser edge, Aubrey tugged the towel off her head and shook her hair around her shoulders.

"That's one thing you forgot, Sara," she said as she turned on the dryer and aimed it at the back of her head. "Food."

Wishing she hadn't given her Big Mac to Jack, Aubrey tried not to listen to the jingle—"Two all-beef patties, special sauce, lettuce, cheese"—that kept running through her head. Quickly she dried her hair, then frowned at the frizzy, recently permed auburn cloud billowing around her face.

"Fetching," she muttered and bent down to unplug the dryer.

Once she'd refolded it and tucked it back in Sara's bag, she peeled the spread off the bed, folded it into a pallet on the floor, tossed a pillow on top of it, and then turned back the sheets for Jack. She could still hear water running in the bathroom, but in the sink now rather than the tub. He's probably shaving, she thought as she repacked Sara's things in her bag. She was eyeing a tube of suntan oil and wondering why Sara had brought it when she heard the hissing, half-strangled groan from the bathroom.

"Jack?" She stuffed the tube back in Sara's purse and swung it onto the floor. "Are you all right?"

"Fine," he answered, but she thought his voice sounded strained. "I, uh, cut myself shaving."

A second later, Aubrey heard the lock click open. Ripping off the towel around her waist, she dove into her pallet and jerked the top half of the spread over her as the door opened.

"Aubrey?" Jack called.

"Down here," she answered and raised her right hand above the bed.

The box springs squeaked, and a second later Jack leaned over the side of the mattress to look at her. He cocked one eyebrow at her curiously and braced his weight on his right elbow.

"What are you doing down there?"

"Sleeping."

"Scout's honor I won't attack you, Dumpling."

He raised his left arm from his side and drew an "X" across his naked chest. As he did, Aubrey gasped at the red-splotched strip of gauze tied to his upper arm.

"How did you cut your arm shaving?"

He glanced down at the bandage, then winced guiltily and tucked his arm behind him.

"Jack." She said his name firmly as she held the spread against her breasts and sat up. "What happened to your arm?"

"It's nothing, really," he assured her. "Just a graze."

"A graze from what?"

"A bullet."

"A *bullet!*" She shrieked and let the spread fall

as she scrambled up on her knees. "Why didn't you tell me!"

"It's only a nick." He swung himself into a sitting position on the side of the bed and caught her shoulders in his hands. "Just a tear in the flesh—it didn't even come close to the muscle. It just hurts and it bleeds a little when I clean it."

"But who shot you?" she asked, her voice trembling as she raised her arms and wrapped her fingers around his wrists.

"Uncle Hugh," he told her with a rueful smile, "only I ducked, broke a beaker over his head, took his gun away from him, and ran like hell."

"The same gun that's in your pocket?"

"The very one." His smile softened and his thumbs softly stroked her bare shoulders.

A shiver laced across her collarbone, and Aubrey, standing on her knees between Jack's legs, lowered her head to hide the flush creeping up her neck. She neglected to close her eyes, however, and they flew wide open, then squeezed tightly shut when she saw that he had nothing on under the towel knotted around his waist.

"Oops, sorry, Dumpling."

He didn't sound the least bit apologetic though, and chuckled as he lifted his right hand from her shoulder. She felt him tug at the sheets, cracked one eye, and saw that he'd drawn the bedclothes over his lap.

"You're breaking your New Year resolution," he said gently as his hand settled on her shoulder again.

"I'm—what?" she asked faintly, her breath coming in shallow gasps.

His eyes were smiling at her now as his hands

moved and cupped her shoulder blades. "You're hyperventilating."

"Oh—no," she breathed, looking away from him as her pulse began to throb in the hollow of her throat. "It's just s-so stuffy in here . . ."

She tried to worm her way out of his grasp, but Jack wouldn't let her go. His hands went to her shoulders again and he drew her closer between his legs. To keep from falling into him, she dropped her hands from his wrists to his knees, and felt the reddish hair covering his skin prickle her fingertips.

"Dumpling, listen to me." He raised his right hand from her shoulder and tipped her chin up on his middle finger. "Just listen and don't interrupt. We got lucky tonight but I've got a bad feeling that things are going to get worse before they get better. The chip is *gone,* and until Sara comes to and can verify my story and tell the cops who drugged her, I've got to stay one jump ahead of the FBI, Nu-Lite, and Hugh Lawrence's goons. Somebody could get hurt, and since I've already seen one person I love end up in the hospital, I'm calling you a taxi first thing in the morning. I want you to go to the airport and grab the first plane headed for Springfield."

"I can't, Jack, I don't have enough money—"

"Yes, you do." He silenced her by raising his finger to her lips. "I went through your purse while you were in the shower."

"That," she accused as her eyes filled slowly with tears, "was a dirty trick."

"I know it was," he said softly, his fingers tracing her bottom lip, "and I'm sorry."

Jerking her head to one side, Aubrey pushed

her hands against his knees, turned awkwardly on her own, and scrambled into her pallet.

"I suppose," she said, her voice quavering as she huddled down on her left shoulder with her back to him and jerked the spread over her, "that you're going to keep my car."

"If you'll let me," Jack said quietly.

"Sure, fine, take it. Just try not to wreck it, okay?" She pushed herself up on her left arm and punched her pillow because she couldn't punch him. "Take the cash too, with my blessing."

"Oh, Jesus, Aubrey," he sighed heavily. "Don't make this any harder for me, will you?"

That was *it.* Grabbing her pillow in her right hand, Aubrey reared up on her tailbone and hurled it at him. He caught it in his left hand and stared at her, open-mouthed.

"Go to hell, Jack!" she shrieked at him. "And have a nice trip!"

Tugging the bedspread with her, she flung herself on her side and pulled it over her head. Curled in a ball, she quaked with fury and misery and bit her lip to quell the sobs tearing at her throat.

"I'm *trying* to protect you, Aubrey."

"Then why"—her voice broke and she drew a deep breath—"why didn't you just leave me in New York? Why did you drag me all this way—"

"Because, goddamnit," Jack broke in angrily, "I'm in love with you. I've been in love with you for years."

"Oh, *sure,* right you are," she said thickly, her tears bleeding into her voice. "You love"—Aubrey's voice stuck in her throat and a slow chill crawled up her back—"*who?*"

"Look, I'm sorry," he said shortly. "I honest to

God never meant to tell you. I got your message a long time ago, Aubrey—you aren't interested—and I really hope this won't louse up our friendship."

"Oh, *Jack*—oh, *God,*" she moaned and rolled over on her stomach to bury her face in her arm.

"I'm sorry, Dumpling," he sighed wearily. "I didn't mean to embarrass you."

The bedsprings squeaked and Aubrey raised her head. Glancing over her left shoulder, she saw him stretched out on his back with his right arm thrown over his eyes.

"Jack?"

"What?"

"I love you."

He raised his arm a little and smiled at her. "I know you do, Dumpling."

"No, you don't understand." Aubrey threw the spread aside, rose to her knees, and leaned her elbows on the bed beside him. "I mean I *love* you."

He raised his arm another inch or so and looked at her steadily. "Say that again," he said slowly.

"I love you," she repeated softly.

Groaning as if in pain, he slid his arm over his eyes and half-rolled away from her. Almost instantly, he rolled back, lowered his arm, and just looked at her.

"You mean to tell me—" he began, then stopped, tipped his head back on the pillow beneath him, and laughed.

Half-afraid that she'd somehow said the wrong thing, Aubrey wilted, inside and out, lowered her chin, and sat back on her heels.

Springing up on the side of the bed, Jack caught her by the shoulders and tugged her up on her knees again. "Don't you dare," he said, drawing her between his legs as he raised his hands and cupped them around her face, "crawl back in that pallet."

"I wasn't going to," she said, her voice and her body trembling at the warmth and gentleness of his touch.

"You're going to sleep with me," he said, smiling as his thumbs lightly stroked her cheekbones, "and we're going to make up for a lot of lost time."

Still holding her face gently between his palms, Jack bent closer to kiss her. This is it, Aubrey thought, her heart yammering in her throat as she closed her eyes and wrapped her fingers around his wrists—The Moment, The Touch . . .

Very lightly his mouth touched hers, parting her lips with a soft moan that quivered up her throat as his arms slipped around her. Beneath her fingers on his wrists, she felt the tremor in his arms as they tightened around her rib cage and he half-lifted, half-pulled her onto the bed. He managed it without breaking the kiss, and she shivered at the heat radiating from his body as he slid down beside her and drew her against him.

"Oh, Aubrey." His mouth pulled reluctantly away from hers, and he sighed her name as he leaned his chin against her forehead and pressed her cheek to his bare chest. "I've dreamed about this, but I never thought it would happen."

"Me either," she murmured, trembling and quaking inside, and wondering what in the world she should do with her hands.

Jack solved part of the problem by catching her

wrist in his hand and pressing her palm against his chest as he leaned away from her and raised himself on his right elbow. Tipping her head back, Aubrey looked up at his face, and her breath caught in her throat. His fingers were still unsteady around her hand and his green eyes were soft and shiny. There were flecks of yellow around his large, dark pupils that she'd never noticed before, and a strawberry flush on his neck.

"I wish I'd listened to Heartburn," he said, smiling ruefully as he lifted her palm and kissed it. "For years she's been telling me that you—"

"Oh, *no,*" Aubrey groaned, and felt a scalding wave of embarrassment wash up her throat.

"You too, huh?"

Swallowing guiltily, Aubrey nodded. "I never believed her," she told him in a small voice.

"Me either," Jack admitted, and his smile quirked sheepishly. "You know, I think we might have made out just fine on our own if she'd left us alone."

"You really think so?"

"No." Jack grinned and laughed. "Because, frankly, Dumpling, I never thought I was anything more to you than Sara's older brother. God, I kept trying to be, but you just wouldn't let me."

"Well, I—" Aubrey's voice failed her, and she shrugged and ducked her head.

"You what?"

"I-I just couldn't face the rejection," she confessed haltingly.

"You never gave me a chance," he reminded her gently.

"I never dreamed you would—or could—" She

paused, drew a deep breath, and looked up at him. "I can't say it," she finished weakly.

"Let me guess." He kissed her palm again and laid it on his chest. "You were self-conscious because you thought you were fat."

*"Thought?"* Aubrey echoed, sounding incredulous and defensive at the same time. "I *was,* Jack. I was *fat.*"

"I never noticed." He made a fist out of his right hand, leaned it against his temple, and smiled.

"Oh, Jack, *really—*"

"I have, however, recently noticed that you're very *un*-fat. I didn't even recognize you at Emily's wedding." His smile softened, and the flush on his throat deepened as his left hand slid slowly off her shoulder. "I'm awfully glad, though, that you haven't lost weight *everywhere.*"

As his hand very lightly cupped her breast Aubrey whimpered and closed her eyes. Oh, Lord, she thought, barely able to breathe as his fingers brushed her stiffening nipple, fantasy never felt like this.

Leaning over her, Jack buried his face in the curve of her neck. His mouth felt as hot as his skin when he kissed her throat and tenderly kneaded her breast with the tips of his fingers.

"Can I talk you out of Sara's nightie?" he asked, his voice deep and hoarse as he raised his head and nipped at her earlobe.

Panic riveted her hands to his shoulders, and her eyes widened as he leaned away from her and arched one eyebrow at her. Somehow her fantasies had never gotten this far, and she wished to

God they had as her heart started thudding in ears.

"I—ah—I'm not very good at this," she confessed and swallowed hard. "I-I haven't had a-a whole lot of experience."

"Don't worry, my love," he said, kissing the tip of her nose as he pulled away from her. "I have."

"I know," Aubrey answered just a tad sourly as she watched him swing off the bed and reach for the lamp on the nightstand. "That's what worries me."

"Relax, Aubrey." Jack glanced at her over his shoulder and smiled as his fingers closed on the switch. "You couldn't disappoint me if you tried."

The lamp clicked off, and Jack was only a tall, dim shape beside the bed until the faint glow from the outside lights bled into the room and her eyes adjusted to the darkness. She caught her breath then and bit back the giddy little whimper in her throat as she watched him untie the towel from his waist and toss it on the foot of the bed.

"I'm not worried about disappointing you," Aubrey confessed in a shaky voice as he slid onto the bed beside her again. "I'm worried about disappointing myself."

"Don't be, my love," he whispered as he leaned over to kiss her. "I won't let you."

He didn't kiss her mouth but the hollow of her throat, and Aubrey moaned at the succulent graze of his lips against her skin. She still wasn't sure what to do with her hands, but slid them tentatively over his shoulders and felt him shiver. A little thrill coursed through her, and she kissed him very lightly on the temple. Another tremor rippled his shoulders, and he made a noise in his throat as she curled her fingers and gently raked her nails across his back.

Happy, astonished tears sprang into her eyes, and Aubrey tightened her arms around Jack's neck as she realized that he wanted her as much as she wanted him. Oh, joy, she thought, oh, *Jack,* and lowered her arms to take his face in her hands and kiss him. She parted her mouth first with a quick flick of her tongue, and felt rather than heard him groan as her moistened lips touched his.

Sliding his arms beneath her, he cupped the back of her head in his hands as he laid her on her back and eased himself on top of her. Her mouth opened wider, trembling, as he slowly rolled his hips over hers and his naked chest brushed her breasts beneath her gown. Feeling her nipples harden and the soft chiffon whisper between them, Aubrey moaned and instinctively arched her back.

Breathing deeply and rapidly, Jack pushed himself up on his knees, caught the hem of her gown, and tugged it gently over her head. Aubrey raised her arms to help, then gasped as he cast it aside and leaned over her again. She moaned and so did he as the hair on his chest curled around her nipples. Cradling her head in his arms again, Jack kissed her mouth, her chin, then her throat and her breasts until he'd kissed every inch of her upper body at least twice, and his lips began to inch lower.

Lost in a haze of desire emanating from the regions Jack seemed intent on exploring now, Aubrey, certain that she'd lose consciousness if he kissed here *there,* laid her hands on his shoulders and drew his lips up to hers. Combing his fingers through her hair, he tilted her head back on the pillow, covered her mouth with his, and gently eased their bodies together.

A small muscle spasm made Aubrey stiffen, but Jack relaxed above her and teased the corner of her mouth with his tongue until he'd smoothed her discomfort away. She kissed him back then, touching the tip of her tongue to his and moaning softly as he moved in slow, small circles against her. Wrapping her arms tightly around his neck, Aubrey closed her eyes and clung to him.

With slow, cherishing strokes he made love to her, murmuring things in her ear that probably would have made her blush if the lights were on. In the dark, however, whispered in a passion-roughened voice, the obscene little words and phrases made her feel beautiful and loved and heightened her desire. She felt no discomfort now, only a warm, lush glow that flushed rapidly through her body and then broke suddenly in a swirl of ecstatic sensations that trapped her breath in her throat and arched her body against Jack. She said his name once, softly, as he spoke hers on a deep intake of breath, and she felt him stiffen above her.

"Oh, Aubrey," he groaned as his arms went lax and his body collapsed on top of hers. "Don't hate me, my love, but I'm gonna fall alseep."

He did, too, almost instantly, with his forehead buried in the pillow and his nose pressed against her temple. A half-second later, he began to snore lightly in her ear.

Burrowed snugly beneath him, Aubrey drew the sheet over his damp shoulder blades, wrapped her arms around him, and closed her eyes. Very softly she cried, and thanked heaven that Jack was already asleep. He just wouldn't have understood.

# Chapter Eleven

THOUGH Aubrey's fantasies had always skipped over the lovemaking, they'd been very clear and explicit about the morning after. She'd always wakened looking like Mary Tyler Moore, with every hair on her head in place, and not one wrinkle in her nightgown. There'd also been a gold wedding band on the third finger of her left hand and an empty magnum of champagne at the bedside, but there'd been absolutely nothing in her dreams about tangled sheets and Jack's very heavy right leg thrown on top of her.

Wondering how in the world she was going to wiggle out from under Jack without waking him, Aubrey turned her head and blinked at him sleepily. The right side of his face was buried in the pillow and he was still snoring, very lightly, with his mouth slightly open. To describe his hair as rumpled would have been an understatement, and she smiled softly as she raised her right hand and smoothed one of the reddish-brown tufts sticking up around his face.

Once before she'd seen his hair in a similar state of disarray, when he'd come down to Columbia, Missouri, to escort Sara and her on a canoe trip down the Current River in the Ozarks. It had been a mandatory field outing for a required course in ecology, and they'd both thought that taking a scientist along (naively, they'd thought any old kind of scientist would do) would be an excellent idea.

Sporting his MIT beard and bursting with woodsy lore, (which he'd bored Sara and her silly with in the car on the drive down), Natty Bumpo Draper had arrived to lead them fearlessly into the wilderness. Four days later they'd limped him out of it with a sprained ankle, poison ivy, and a hairdo that Sara had said made him look like a startled squirrel. They'd both laughed until they'd cried, but Jack hadn't thought it was the least bit funny.

Remembering, Aubrey's smile quavered and tears prickled in the corners of her eyes. If only Sara were here, she thought (well, not exactly *right* here), if only she'd believed her about Jack. There were no guarantees, yet Aubrey couldn't shake the feeling that if she and Jack had only found each other earlier they wouldn't be in the mess they were in right now. That thought made her remember the truck and the gunshots, made her shiver and decide that it was time for Jack to wake up.

"Jack." She cupped his left shoulder in her right hand and shook him. "Jack, wake up."

His eyebrows drew together and he groaned.

"Jack, *c'mon.*" She shook him a little harder. "It's morning, wake up."

He groaned again, rolled his face into the pillow, and moved his right leg. For that Aubrey was grateful, but her relief changed rapidly to dismay when he started snoring again, louder this time, and burrowed himself deeper into the pillow.

This wouldn't do. Her Timex said eight-twenty. They had to get up and get out of here. Aubrey couldn't put her finger on why, she simply knew they *must,* and muttered at him in disgust as she crawled around the bed looking for Sara's nightie. She found it on the floor and tugged it over her head as she rounded the bed and dropped to her knees beside Jack.

"Wake up, Rip Van Winkle," she said loudly into his ear.

She backed out of his way, just barely in time to avoid being whacked in the chin as he shot up on his arms. His eyes were open but unfocused, he groaned again, then he shook his head and blinked at her. Stifling a yawn, he drew up his knees, almost fell over as he sat up, and folded his legs under him.

"Morning," he said groggily as he bent his right elbow on his knee, leaned his head in his hand, and let his eyelids drift shut.

"*Please* wake up, Jack," Aubrey pleaded as she wrapped her hands around his forearm and tried to tug his hand out from under his head. She couldn't budge it.

"I will, I will," he said thickly. "Just give me a minute."

"We don't *have* a minute," she wanted to shriek at him, but for the life of her she couldn't understand why she felt that way. Morning-after jitters, she supposed.

"Wake *up,* Jack," she told him in her best classroom authoritarian voice. "It's almost eight-thirty, we've got to *go.*"

"In a minute, Dumpling." He yawned again, and his head drooped against his hand.

Aubrey decided she had two options—yell *fire* or throw cold water in his face. Since the first one seemed less likely to make him mad, she reared up on her knees and bellowed *"Fire!"* at the top of her lungs. Jack's head drooped lower and he snored louder.

"Okay, fine"—she glared at him as she got to her feet and started toward the bathroom—"but don't yell at me when you're soaking wet."

Snatching up a clear plastic glass from the sink, Aubrey turned on the cold tap and muttered in disgust when the water ran tepid. The hot tap ran hotter, so she carried her glass to the tub and cranked the cold tap on full blast. Too late, she saw that the shower tab was still pulled up, and she shrieked as a spray of icy water drenched the back of her neck.

Peeling her dripping hair out of her face, Aubrey yanked a towel off the edge of the tub and turned around just as Jack yelled her name and came lurching, still half-asleep and naked, through the bathroom door.

"Oh, Jesus," he sighed, sagging on his right shoulder against the doorjamb as he raked his left hand through his hair. "You scared me half to death, Dumpling."

"Well, at least you're awake," Aubrey grumbled as she draped the towel over her wet head and bent forward to dry her hair and hide the flush coloring her cheeks at the sight of his body.

"What happened?" he asked around a yawn.

"You left the shower on," she told him as she rubbed vigorously at her scalp.

"Sorry, Dumpling."

She saw his knees fold onto the bathmat in front of her a second or two before his fingers closed over hers on the towel. He kissed the back of her right hand, then raised her face and kissed her mouth.

"Morning, my love," he said softly as he put his arms around her and pulled her down against him.

This wasn't exactly her fantasy, but close enough to make Aubrey sigh happily and slip her arms around his bare rib cage. He kissed her temple and rubbed his palms up and down her back.

"Know what's my favorite thing to do first thing in the morning?" he asked her, his voice low and close to her ear.

"Eat breakfast, I hope," she answered. "I'm starving."

"That's second." He chuckled. "First is make love in the shower."

His lips brushed her temple again and she shivered as he stood up and drew her with him. "Let me take off your gown," he whispered as he dragged his mouth slowly across hers.

"Jack," she breathed, closing her hands on his wrists as he tugged at Sara's nightie. "Shouldn't we go—"

"Shhh," he said and kissed her as he swept Sara's chiffon gown over her head.

She shivered again, not from cold but nervousness and embarrassment, and squeezed her eyes tightly shut. Any second now he's going to laugh, she thought, but he didn't. He made a noise in his throat that was half-moan and half-groan, and raised her lowered chin to kiss her as he drew her into his arms again.

"You're beautiful, Dumpling," he said in her ear, "what little of you there is."

She opened her eyes then, a defiant glare on her face, and saw that he was grinning at her.

"I thought that'd get you to look at me," he said and massaged his palms on her shoulder blades. "Don't be shy, Aubrey, I love you."

"I love you too," she told him, staring steadfastly at his face.

Curving his right hand around her cheek, he smiled as he bent his head and softly kissed her mouth. "I've always thought you were beautiful," he told her gently.

"Is that why you call me Dumpling?" she asked, her eyelids fluttering shut as he kissed the line of her jaw.

"As a matter of fact," he answered, his words slurred as he dragged his mouth down the curve of her throat, "yes."

Cold spray splashed over the side of the tub, splattering the backs of her knees and making her shiver in earnest. Her teeth began to chatter, and she was about to say something to Jack when he raised his head from the curve of her neck, kissed the tip of her nose lightly, and turned toward the tub to adjust the shower. Doing her best to cover her body with her arms, Aubrey backed out of the way and watched him step into the tub, draw the curtain aside, and hold his hand out to her.

Her fingers trembled as she laid her left hand in his, and he helped her over the side of the tub. Gooseflesh sprang on her body at the warm pulse of the shower beating on her back, and Jack made that funny moaning-groaning noise in his throat as he drew her against him and embraced her. Wrapping her arms around his rib cage, Aubrey laid her cheek on his chest and sighed as his soapy hands worked up and down her back.

"I think I fell in love with you the first time I saw you," he said, his voice low and gentle in her ear as his fingers kneaded the back of her neck. "You looked so terrified when Heartburn threw open the door to your dormitory room and announced that she was your roommate."

"I *was* terrified," Aubrey admitted, lifting her head to smile at him as she freed one hand from his waist to smooth her dripping hair out of her eyes. "I'd been in a state of panic for weeks, anyway, about who was going to be my roommate, and then in walked this svelte, sophisticated creature, and I just *knew* she was going to hate me."

"Did you even see me, Dumpling?"

"Not right away." Aubrey wrinkled her nose at him. "I mean, you were buried under all that luggage."

Jack chuckled and rested his jaw against her forehead as his hands rubbed circles on the small of her back. "So what *did* you think when you got a good look at me?"

"I don't remember that I thought much of anything," Aubrey confessed, moving her fingers experimentally on his back. "I was sort of overwhelmed when Sara told me you were a senior at Cornell and that you'd been accepted at MIT for your graduate work. I think I did notice that you were tall."

"Tall?" He leaned away from her and shook his

streaming hair out of his face. "That was *it?* You noticed I was *tall?*"

"I wasn't very sure of myself, Jack," she reminded him, "and men terrified me. I tried to pretend that you weren't there and I kept praying that you'd leave."

"Oh, but I was having so much fun helping you and Heartburn rearrange the furniture and hang up all Sara's antiwar posters." He grinned at her and snuggled her closer. "And truthfully, Dumpling, I could tell I was making you nervous and I loved it. I thought, Hot dog, she's crazy about me." His grin dimmed a little. "It was a real kick in the ego when I realized you weren't."

"Oh, but I was by three o'clock," she assured him quickly. "By then I'd noticed that you were handsome as well as tall, and very bright and very funny, and that you loved Sara a lot and I"—her voice cracked a little as she thought about Sara—"and I wished you felt that way about me."

"All that money my parents spent on Cornell and MIT." Jack sighed and shook his head.

Aubrey tilted her chin curiously to one side. "Huh?"

"I'd say it was a waste, wouldn't you?" He looked down at her and smiled. "All that education and I wasn't smart enough to see through your gigantic inferiority complex."

"You're a physicist," she reminded him as she lightly kissed his chin, "not a psychiatrist. And you weren't the one with the weight problem, I was. It was so simple once I tumbled to it—all I had to do was stop stuffing brownies in my face."

Laughing, Jack hugged her tighter, then leaned her away from him and frowned at her sternly. "It wasn't just the brownies, Dumpling, and you know it," he told her. "Bless your mother's dictatorial little heart—"

"She thinks very highly of you too," Aubrey interrupted with a laugh.

"I like your mother, I really do," Jack assured her quickly, then turned his head to one side and looked at her askance. "She's the one who gave you the Mace, isn't she?"

"How did you know?"

"I've met your mother, Aubrey, several times." His smile twisted ruefully. "Just in case, I think I'll hang on to the Mace. I have a feeling I'm going to need it when we tell her about us."

"Tell her what?"

How, over the roar of the shower, Aubrey managed to hear the door open she was never sure—but she did, and so did Jack, whose smile suddenly vanished as his head jerked toward the bedroom. Clutching at his slippery skin with shaking fingers, Aubrey too glanced toward the doorway and felt her heart freeze between her ribs.

Through the opaque plastic curtain she saw the dim shapes of two men standing just outside the bathroom. One was very tall and broad-shouldered, and by comparison, the other looked almost short.

"Good morning, Jack. Can I buy you and your lady some breakfast?"

The voice was well modulated and pleasant, but it made Aubrey shiver. She felt the tremor crawl across her shoulders, and Jack's arms tightened around her.

"No thanks, John," he answered smoothly. "We're really not hungry."

"Oh, but I think you should eat, Jack." The man paused. "After all, this may be your last chance."

A startled, panicked gasp escaped her before Jack silenced her with his hand over her mouth. Wide-eyed, she sucked air through her nose and stared up at him. Gently, he lifted his hand, pursed his lips, and pressed his index finger to his mouth.

"Why do you say *may,* John?" He reversed their positions, leaned over to shut off the water, then pulled a towel off the rack secured to the back wall of the tub and draped it around her. "I've never known you to be indecisive."

"I just thought I'd give you one last chance to turn the chip over to me."

"What chip?" Jack asked, raking his wet hair out of his face with his hands.

"Really, Jack." The man sighed impatiently, and Aubrey shivered as she wrapped the towel around her body, and pulled a second one off the rack. "The one Jeb sent you, and please don't lie about it. We found the package receipt in his apartment."

"I don't have it, John." Jack took the towel Aubrey offered him with a shaking hand and knotted it around his waist. "I lost it at Hugh Lawrence's lab."

"Nice try, Jack; unfortunately, I don't believe you."

As Aubrey watched their shadows beyond the curtain, she saw the smaller man lift one arm. A second later she heard a metallic click and nearly jumped out of her towel.

"Everybody out, Jack. You first."

Lifting his right arm, Jack swept his hand behind Aubrey's neck and kissed her. "Don't panic," he whispered as he drew away from her. "We may get out of this yet."

He drew the curtain aside, stepped out of the tub, and drew it shut behind him.

"Now you, Miss Nichols."

A shiver crawled up her back as he said her name. She moved to comply, but Jack reached behind him with one hand and held the curtain shut.

"Why don't we step into the other room and give her a chance to dress while we discuss this," he suggested. "There aren't any windows in here, she won't go anyplace."

"Always the gallant." The man chuckled. "All right, get her clothes."

Trembling violently inside her towel, Aubrey held her breath as she watched the smaller man follow Jack out of the bathroom. The large, broad shadow remained in the open doorway until Jack's tall, lean shape reappeared and hung something over the towel rack by the sink.

"Get dressed, Aubrey," he said quietly and pulled the door shut behind him.

In a flash she raked the curtain aside and all but jumped out of the tub and across the room to trip the lock on the knob. On the other side of the door she heard a deep, throaty chuckle that she guessed came from the lumbering shadow. Trying desperately not to cry and to listen to the muted voices in the bedroom, Aubrey pulled off her towel and dried her body. Underneath Sara's shorts and blouse, she found the clean pair of lavender panties and her bra, which she hurriedly hooked herself into. Her fingers shook so hard she could barely pull on the underpants and shorts, and buttoning the buttons was almost impossible. She'd nearly managed to worry the top button through its hole when a sharp rap at the door made her jump and lose her grip on the plaid cotton madras.

"Quickly, Miss Nichols," the man named John said. "You're holding up breakfast."

"I-I'm coming," she stammered. "Just a moment."

Frozen in front of the mirror, she listened over the roar of the blood in her ears as he moved away from the door. Her knees went weak then, and she sagged against the edge of the sink on her hands. Oh, God, she moaned silently, if only she had the Mace canister.

Dragging the back of her hand across her tear-blurred eyes, Aubrey raised her head and looked at her pale, chalky reflection. Don't just stand here, she told herself, *do* something. Sara wouldn't just stand here, she'd think of something. . . . Looking past her left shoulder in the mirror, Aubrey's eyes widened suddenly as she saw a can of Lysol spray sitting on the back corner of the bathtub.

It isn't Mace, she thought as she quickly darted across the room and leaned over the tub to retrieve it, but it *is* an eye irritant. Holding the can in her shaking arm, she read the label—"Avoid direct spraying into eyes"—and looked around frantically for a way to hide it. Her eyes fell on the towel she'd dropped on the floor in front of the sink, and she bent hurriedly and snatched it up.

She draped it over her shoulders, tucked the can of Lysol in her right hand underneath it, and held the towel closed in her left fist. As she moved toward the door, she peeked under the wet terrycloth rectangle and made sure the arrow on the spray cap and her index finger were pointing in the right direction—away from her.

With any luck, only the big man would have a gun, and if he were still lurking near the door—Oh, God, please, she prayed as her clammy fingers slipped on the doorknob, oh, *please* just let there be one gun.

As she tripped the lock the door sprang inward. Startled, she leaped away from it and gaped, wide-eyed, at the monstrous shadow she'd seen through the shower curtain. In the flesh he was terrifying, a big burly man who bore an uncanny resemblance to a grizzly bear. With one hand on the doorknob, he pushed the door open and looked at her. At her bare legs, anyway, and she felt her stomach turn as his small, close-together brown eyes traveled up the length of her body.

She'd never seen a leer before—not directed at her, anyway—but Aubrey recognized the one on his face as his gaze came to rest on her hand clutched around the towel. Her stomach stopped pitching and she gritted her teeth in disgust.

"What's under the towel, honey?"

He asked, so Aubrey showed him. His eyes widened briefly as she thrust the can in his face and pressed the spray cap. He made one swipe at her as a cloud of mist enveloped his head, but she ducked it by dodging past him through the doorway. Very briefly, as she swung around to keep an eye on the lurching, lumbering bear, she saw Jack jump the man named John from behind. She heard a crash, whirled, and saw the big man on the floor, his back against the desk, his eyes streaming tears as he groped for a handhold to pull himself up.

That she couldn't allow. Darting toward him as he lowered both his hands, she gave him another shot of Lysol full in the face, then leaped away as he roared and lurched up on his knees. Blind as he was, he threw his arms open to grab her, lost his balance, and pitched forward. His head hit the steel bed frame with a sickening thud, and he sprawled face first on the carpet.

A hand fell between her shoulder blades and, shrieking, Aubrey pivoted, her Lysol can raised. The spray cap hissed, but Jack grabbed her wrist and shoved her arm over her head as he swept his left arm around her and hugged her.

"Oh, Jack," she sobbed and sagged against him, light-headed and shaking.

"Watch him." He nodded at a second prone figure lying facedown on the floor as he pulled away from her. "If he so much as breathes heavy, *squirt* him."

He bolted away from her to the bed and started yanking off the sheets. Biting her bottom lip between her teeth and aiming the Lysol can at the floor, she crept toward the still form of a blond man in a powder blue suit and kept watch while Jack ripped strips of sheet and bent over the unconscious bear.

"Is this guy John Collins?" she asked, moving nervously from one foot to the other as she kept the can trained on him.

"Yes, my love," Jack, out of sight on the floor, grunted a little. "That's him, the dirty SOB."

"I hope we're going to call the police now."

"And tell them what?"

"What do you *mean,* tell them what? They broke in here with guns and threatened to kill us—"

"What gun?" Jack interrupted, tearing off the towel drooping around his waist as he strode past her and knelt beside Collins with three strips of torn linen in his hands.

"I heard *something* click—"

"What you heard"—he glanced up at her and nodded at the trussed bear—"was Frank over there, head of Nu-Lite security, playing with his brass knuckles. He doesn't need guns to hurt people, my love." He shot her another quick look as he tugged Collins's limp arms behind his back. "And the police want *me* too, Dumpling."

"Oh." She sighed unhappily and flushed. "I'm sorry, I'd almost forgotten."

"That's encouraging." He flashed her a quick smile as he knotted the cloth sheets around Collins's wrists and moved down to his ankles. "Get the keys, Aubrey—they're in my jacket—start the car and back it out. I'll be finished here in a minute."

Taking time only to put on her espadrilles, she did as she was told. Her wet hair dripped down the back of her neck, but it felt good in the bright, steamy morning that had dawned after last night's storm. At the touch of the key in the ignition, the Camaro's engine kicked over with a throaty roar, and the tires spit gravel as she put the Z-28 in reverse and backed it out of the carport. As she turned the car around Jack came pelting out of the cottage in his running shorts and Cornell T-shirt, with her purse in one hand, Sara's in the other, and his jacket, clothes, and her sweater and clamdiggers draped over his arms. In one swift move he opened the door, leaped into the passenger seat, and shut it behind him.

"Get us out of here, Dumpling," he said as he pitched the handbags and his jacket into the backseat and slid down on his spine. "Take a left when you hit the road."

With Indianapolis 500-winning form, Aubrey changed gears, clutched, and rocketed the Z-28 out of the graveled yard. The left turn she made was a little too tight, but she straightened the nose of the car quickly and it shot smoothly down the road. Following Jack's directions, she pushed the Camaro down countless back roads and country lanes. She rolled down her window and so did he, while the Z-28 tore over ancient bridges and along orchard-lined byways heavy with the smells of ripening fruit. Apples Aubrey thought, and bit her lip as her stomach growled pathetically.

She hadn't any idea how many miles they'd put between themselves and the two unconscious men in the motel room when her hands began to tremble on the wheel. The tremor spread rapidly up her arms, and Jack, who'd been as silent as she, leaned toward her and lightly kissed the right side of her neck.

"Pull over, Dumpling, I'll drive," he said.

By the time she'd nosed the car onto the narrow, rutted shoulder, her shakes had spread to her legs, and her knees almost buckled under her as she opened her door and got out of the Camaro to trade places with Jack. He caught her in his arms in front of the car, crushed her against him, and rained kisses on her forehead and ears.

"You were wonderful," he said, leaning her

away from him to cup her face in his hands. "If you hadn't thought of the Lysol, we probably would've ended up as Frank's breakfast."

"I know." She wrapped her arms around him and suppressed a shudder. "I don't think I've ever been so scared in my whole life."

"Me either," Jack sighed and hugged her closer. "Thank God the money your mother spent on *your* education wasn't a waste."

There was just a little twinge of bent ego in his voice, and Aubrey pried herself off his chest to look up at him. He was smiling at her, and she noticed that her shakes had stopped.

"I just tried to think like Sara," she told him.

His smile faded a little. He kissed her quickly, then pushed her gently toward the passenger side of the car. Once they were both in their seats and the Camaro was tracking rapidly down the road again, Jack lifted his right hand from the gearshift and laid it over her right knee.

"As soon as we find a phone, Dumpling," he announced firmly, "we're going to call the hospital and check up on old Heartburn."

"Do you think that's wise?"

"Probably not." He cast her a rueful smile. "But I feel like hell that we had to leave her like that."

"I do too," she agreed and laid her hand over Jack's. "You can't send me home now, you know," she told him. "Collins knows my name, and if he and Frank—"

"I wouldn't worry about them, Dumpling," he interrupted, and his fingers squeezed hers. "We neglected to take the key back, which means any old time now the manager will be checking up on number seven. He'll call the police, I've no doubt."

That gladdened Aubrey's heart, but only briefly. "I'm not going, Jack," she said, her voice quiet but firm. "I'm staying with you."

"Well, of course you are."

"I mean it, I won't—" She caught her breath and bounced sideways in her seat to look at him. He was grinning at her. "What changed your mind?"

"What do *you* think?"

He cocked one eyebrow at her and Aubrey flushed. Her stomach quivered giddily, and with her fingers laced through Jack's, she sighed back in her seat and savored being desirable. It was a wonderful feeling, she decided, much more satisfying than brownies.

# Chapter Twelve

By ten o'clock, both Aubrey and the Camaro were ravenous, she for food and the Z-28 for unleaded premium. When she told Jack she was going to be sick if she didn't eat something soon, he barely muttered a reply and frowned at the gas gauge. Just a bit grudgingly, Aubrey thought he might be more concerned about her needs if she had a five-speed transmission and two hundred and fifty horses under her hood.

"I'm not trying to be a pest," she insisted and clutched her gnawingly empty stomach, "but I haven't had a decent meal since the night before last."

"Uh-huh," he agreed absently as he looked up at the road and then back at the gas gauge again.

She had a feeling he hadn't heard a word she'd said and tried another tack. "Your shorts are on fire, Jack."

"Hmmm," he murmured, his eyebrows knitting together.

Normally a nonviolent person, Aubrey made a fist out of her left hand, raised it—but Jack reached across the console and closed his hand around hers before she could land the punch she had aimed at his arm.

"Down girl," he said, glancing her a smile. "If we're on the road I think we're on, there should be a gas station and a little store about a mile or so ahead. If we're not"—he squeezed her hand, then let it go and wrapped his fingers around the shifter knob—"then we're going to be pushing the car."

"*You* will be pushing the car," she corrected him tartly. "*I* will be sitting here eating my espadrilles."

He chuckled, then whooped happily as the Camaro slid around a curve in the road and a squat stone building sitting in the middle of a tree-shaded lot came into view. The Z-28 hiccupped and bucked once within ten yards of the drive, then kicked again as it made the turn. With a last, shuddery cough, the engine died, and the Camaro rolled up to the pumps in front of the building.

"Do I have great timing or what?" Jack grinned at her as he shut the key off and pulled it out of the ignition.

"What you have," Aubrey replied as she turned on her knees and reached between the seats to retrieve her purse, "is phenomenal luck."

"There is no such thing as luck." He laid his right index finger on the tip of her nose as she straightened out of the backseat. "Ask me, I'm a physicist."

Crossing her eyes at him, Aubrey stuck out her tongue and turned around to open her door. Jack chuckled and shoved his shoulder against the driver's side door. They met on the stone-paved island, and Aubrey cast a dubious frown at the pumps as she pulled her wallet out of her purse and opened it.

"Do they work?" she asked him. "I've seen pictures of these in *The Smithsonian* magazine."

"Look at the price per gallon." Jack pointed at it as he lifted the hose from the unleaded premium pump.

"You're right," she said, and shaded her eyes with her left hand as she handed Jack a twenty. "Where's this store you were telling me about?"

"Right inside," he told her as he dragged the hose around the back of the car. "Get something for me too, would you?"

"No, I'm going to let you starve." Aubrey wrinkled her nose at him and slithered between two antique-looking pumps toward the door.

The interior of the little stone building was dim and cool, and through a screen door in the back paneled wall, Aubrey saw, as she entered, a portly little man rise from a rocking chair and lay a newspaper back in the seat. He waved as he ambled toward her, and she smiled briefly, then turned her attention to the shelves lining the small room and the cooler in the back.

In less than five minutes, she'd spent twenty-four dollars and filled two brown paper sacks. She'd half-filled a third and bought a bag of ice and a Styrofoam cooler to hold the two six-packs of Diet Coke she'd added to her bill, when Jack stepped inside to pay for the gas.

The pudgy little man, who hadn't said a word the whole time Aubrey had been in the store, grinned suddenly and thanked them both profusely in a squeaky little voice. He gave her the change, and Jack scooped up two of the sacks and the cooler.

"I think you made his day," Jack chuckled at her as they carried the groceries to the car.

"I know I made mine." She sighed happily, opened the passenger door, and folded the bucket seat forward.

"You want all this in there?" Jack cocked one eyebrow at her. "Dumpling, we're only two people and you must have enough food here for a week."

"At least," she agreed as she bent forward and tucked the cooler on the floor, "I'm not going to go hungry again."

While Jack dumped the ice in the cooler Aubrey pulled the cans of Diet Coke out of their plastic rings and pushed them to the bottom. That done, they loaded the sacks on the backseat and got into the car, and Jack drove it away from the pumps toward the telephone booth.

"Want to call Heartburn now?"

"Oh, *yes,*" Aubrey sighed happily.

Once he'd stopped the car, Aubrey opened her door and followed him with her wallet from the Camaro to the phone booth. They crowded into it together, and she fed money into the coinbox while Jack placed the call through the operator.

"Ask for patient information first and go from there," he said as he handed her the receiver.

She nodded, and did so once the operator answered. A moment or two later, another woman came on the line and Aubrey asked if she could tell her the condition of Sara Draper, who'd been admitted (she hoped) the previous night.

"One moment, please," the pleasantly nasal voice replied, and Aubrey held up one finger to

Jack. "Ms. Draper is listed in satisfactory condition."

"Oh, thank God," Aubrey sighed.

"Her room number is two-oh-four," the voice went on. "May I connect you?"

Quickly, Aubrey pressed her hand over the mouthpiece. "Want to ring her room?"

"You bet." Jack grinned.

She took her hand off the receiver and said eagerly, "You bet."

"One moment please."

A second or two later, Aubrey heard another ring on the line, then a click as the phone was lifted from its cradle. Her heart leaped in her breast, then plummeted to the soles of her feet as a deep, gruff male voice said, "Felix O'Malley."

Covering the mouthpiece again, she pivoted toward Jack. "It's O'Malley," she whispered in a shaky voice.

"I don't care if it's the devil himself," Jack answered in a low voice. "Ask how she is, then hang up."

"O'Malley here, who is this?" The FBI man barked as she uncovered the mouthpiece and cleared her throat.

"H-hi there, Mr. O'Malley," she said brightly. "This is Aubrey Nichols. How's Sara?"

"W-e-l-l-l." He drew the one-syllable word out slowly. "Is your hair dry yet, Miss Nichols?"

"Almost." She tried to laugh but failed. "Please, Mr. O'Malley, how's Sara?"

"Coming around—slowly, but she's coming around. She keeps mumbling something about pearls. You wouldn't happen to know what she's talking about, would you, Miss Nichols?"

"N-no, I'm afraid not," Aubrey stammered, stepping closer to Jack as he wrapped his hand over hers on the receiver to listen. "She's going to be all right, isn't she?"

"The doctor says she'll be fine, and if you want to stay the same way, young woman, I'd talk Dr. Draper into turning himself in if I were you. It's the best shot he has—"

At the tinny, metallic click on the line, Jack snatched the receiver out of her hand and slammed it down.

"Tapped," he said, then caught her hand and tugged her out of the phone booth behind him.

"Do you think we were on long enough to trace it?" Aubrey asked, half-running behind him back to the car.

"I don't know." Jack flung his door open and slid behind the wheel. "But we aren't going to hang around long enough to find out."

In the few seconds it took Aubrey to let herself into the Camaro, Jack had started the engine and slipped the transmission into first gear. As she shut her door behind her he hit the clutch, and the Camaro shot out onto the road.

"And now we eat," Aubrey said eagerly as she turned on her knees, leaned between the seats, and tugged a sack of goodies into the front seat with her.

For twenty minutes, she and Jack stuffed themselves, beginning with Vienna sausage, Colby cheese and Hi-Ho crackers. This they followed with two apples and a banana, topped off with a package of Hostess Sno-balls.

Chuckling at her as she leaned back in her seat, Jack leaned toward her and smacked a quick kiss on the side of her mouth. He straightened then behind the wheel and smiled at her with coconut in the corner of his mouth.

"Now you're the Aubrey Nichols I fell in love with."

"Watch it," she warned as she stretched toward him to kiss him back. "I'm still very sensitive about food jokes. How about a Coke?"

"Tepid or not, I'd love one."

"Me too," she said and wiggled between the seats again to open the cooler. "Jack," she asked as she pulled two cans out of the ice and handed one to him, "not that I'm not enjoying this scenic tour of the back roads of upstate New York, but where are we going?"

"Canada, my love," he told her as she settled back in her seat. "Via Niagara."

"Just to see the Falls?"

"Hardly." He grinned. "It's only about a three-hour drive, and it's occurred to me that we should be able to hang out there in relative safety—at least from the FBI—until Heartburn comes around and can clear my good name."

Aubrey pulled the ring on her Coke and looked at him for a moment. "I'm not trying to burst your bubble, Jack, but how's she going to do that without the chip?"

"Figured that out, did you?" He glanced sideways at her and frowned. She nodded and he sighed. "There's that risk, Dumpling, that no one will believe her."

"I know that, but what does it mean?"

"It means"—he took a swig of his Coke and looked at her briefly—"that if your friend O'Malley doesn't buy Sara's story, I'd better learn to speak French."

"*We* had better learn to speak French," she corrected him.

"No, Aubrey." Jack smiled but his voice was firm. "There's a distinct possibility here that I could end up semi-permanently on the lam—"

"Then so do I," she maintained. "What kind of a life would I have without you? Besides, you're the one who told me O'Malley could get me for aiding and abetting a fugitive."

"And probably would," Jack agreed grimly. "How *exactly* did he say Sara is?"

"Coming around slowly," Aubrey told him, "and mumbling something about pearls."

"Pearls?" Jack glanced her a quizzical frown.

"Don't ask me." Aubrey shrugged. "I can't imagine what it means."

"Probably nothing," Jack sighed as he bent his left elbow on the door. "She's hallucinating, more than likely. Is she going to be all right?"

"According to O'Malley, the doctor said she's going to be fine."

"Until she finds out we went to Canada without her." Dragging his hand through his wind-dried hair, Jack cast her a brief smile. "Then we'll probably have Heartburn on our trail too."

The thought of Sara lying in a sterile white bed mumbling about pearls made it impossible for Aubrey to smile back at him. She tried but just couldn't muster enough enthusiasm to lift the corners of her mouth.

"This isn't exactly a happy ending, is it?" Jack asked, sighing, as he fixed his eyes on the road.

"It's not your fault," Aubrey murmured. "I just

keep thinking about Sara. Do you think Collins was the one who drugged her?"

"I don't think so, Dumpling. While you were getting dressed, I tried to lead him into admitting it, but he wouldn't bite. I think that was genuine. John Collins has always been many things, but he's never been a very accomplished liar—he takes too much pleasure in reciting his nastier exploits."

"How in the world," Aubrey asked, turning sideways in her seat, "did you end up working for a man like that?"

"In a word, my love, money." Jack shot her a twisted, glum frown. "Nu-Lite offered me big bucks. Not in terms of salary so much, though that was nice, but for financing my research. There never seems to be enough money for research, but Nu-Lite had bags of it lying around, and since my ego couldn't take much more in the way of rejection, I decided San Diego and Nu-Lite was the place for me. It took me a while to tumble to what kind of guy John was, but by then Jeb and I were heavy into the LC-15, and the last thing I wanted to do was turn *that* over to him."

"But if Collins didn't drug Sara, and he doesn't have the chip, then that means Lawrence has it, right?"

"Probably," Jack agreed glumly, "and that scares me almost as much as the thought of it falling into John's hands. I'm almost beginning to hope that there really *is* some foreign government lurking around trying to filch it."

"I don't suppose you can tell me what the LC-15 is, can you?"

"No, Dumpling, I can't, but suffice it to say that it's sort of a Jekyll-Hyde thing. It could be very good or very, *very* bad, and what scares me about Hugh getting hold of it is the fact that he's desperate. His lab is about to go down the tubes—I've been hearing rumors for months, and he told me so himself—and desperate men sometimes do some pretty crazy things."

"He couldn't, like . . . blow up the world with it or anything, could he?" Aubrey asked nervously.

"Oh, hell, no." Jack grinned at her and chuckled. "Maybe just half of it."

"You're kidding, right?"

"Of course I'm kidding." His grin faded and he shook his head. "Why, I don't know, but I *am* kidding."

With the Camaro cruising along in fifth gear, he lifted his hand from the gearshift and laced his fingers through Aubrey's. She smiled at him, then leaned her head back against her seat and looked out the window. Outside it was a beautiful green and gold summer day, but inside she felt like crying.

"There's something you've never told me, Dumpling. How did you get to commencement?"

He didn't say which commencement, baccalaureate or master's, but he didn't have to. Aubrey knew exactly which one he meant, and his question gave her a start.

"I walked," she told him.

"You *what?*"

"I walked." She shifted toward him in her seat again and smiled at the incredulous expression on his face. "How else was I supposed to get there?"

"Why didn't you call your mother at her motel?" He glanced at Aubrey, then back at the road. "Never mind, that was a dumb question."

"I didn't mind," Aubrey said, turning her head to look out the window again. "The exercise did me good."

"I went back for you."

"You *did?*" She turned quickly back to him.

"Sure I did." He tightened his fingers on hers. "I damn near died when you came down the steps with Heartburn and you looked at the car. If I'd only thought . . ." He glanced at her briefly, then back at the road. "But then—you didn't think either, Dumpling."

"What do you *mean,* I didn't? I knew the minute I saw that Volkswagen—"

"Sara was going to ride in the back."

He said it very quietly and without emphasis. Her lips parted of their own volition, and Aubrey simply stared at him.

"She and I had it all arranged." He gave her another quick, sideways glance. "The only thing we forgot to do was tell *you.* I wish we'd thought of that."

"So do I," Aubrey murmured, and blinked back tears that she turned her head toward the window to hide.

"That isn't quite all we arranged," Jack went on. "At Easter vacation, you know, when you went back to Springfield for your interview at the Peterson School?"

"Oh, yes," Aubrey answered as she lifted her right hand, surreptitiously she hoped, and wiped at her eyes with her fingertips. "I remember."

"Well." Jack drew a deep breath and then sighed. "Heartburn and I went shopping and I bought you a ring. I had the boot of the VW all packed . . . Sara'd been stealing clothes out of your closet for weeks—"

"That *sneak!*" Aubrey whirled, wide-eyed, away from the window. "She told me the laundry had lost my things!"

"She lied. She took them, packed a suitcase—"

"Where were we going?"

Jack looked at her again and drew another deep breath. "To Miami, Oklahoma, to get married. They have those 'instant wedding' chapels there."

"Uh-huh." Aubrey nodded. "And who's idea was that, as if I didn't know?"

"It was only *half* her idea," Jack added quickly.

"Which half?"

"The half where we got you drunk at the party that night, poured you in the car, and drove you to Oklahoma to say 'I do' before you sobered up enough to realize what you were doing."

"Why didn't you *ask* me?"

"Why haven't I done a lot of things?" He shrugged a little and raked his fingers through his hair again. "You want the truth?"

"It's slightly after the fact, but why not?"

"Because I was scared to death you'd say no."

"Oh, *Jack.*" Aubrey's voice warbled a little as more tears welled in her eyes. "You sound like me."

"We *do* have an awful lot in common." He shot her a quirky smile and squeezed her fingers again. "I'm not nearly as comfortable with women as I am with petri dishes and microscopes—electron or otherwise."

"Oh, *really?*" she taunted with a raised eyebrow. "You aren't, but your alter-ego John Reed is, huh?" She tsked at him. "And you told *me* not to use a generic name."

"It's not generic, that's my first and middle name." He smiled at her, a half-apologetic, half-wicked little smile. "You won't believe this, but I *did* try to save myself for you, Dumpling."

"You're right," she agreed matter-of-factly. "I don't believe you."

"I said I *tried,*" Jack repeated, his smile taking a definite swing to the wicked side.

"Obviously," Aubrey replied, trying to sound haughty, "you didn't try hard enough."

"I *did,*" Jack insisted, making a fist out of his right hand and pounding it against the steering wheel for emphasis. "I tried *Playboy* and cold showers—"

"Is that how you ended up with a fiancée?"

Jack slid her a puzzled glance. "What fiancée?"

"Mary Elizabeth Something-or-Other," Aubrey reminded him. "I can't remember—"

"Oh, Jesus." Jack winced and smacked his palm against his forehead. "That one *was* Heartburn's idea. Totally and completely. I didn't know anything about it, I swear to God I didn't—"

"You mean"—Aubrey sucked a furious breath, then let it out in one big puff—"she made it up?"

Jack nodded. "She made it up."

"She made it *up,*" Aubrey repeated incredulously and balled her fists in her lap. "I'll *kill* her!"

"You have to admit, Dumpling," Jack put in sagely, "we definitely needed help."

"I'm *still* going to kill her," Aubrey vowed.

"Do you want your ring?"

"Ring?" she echoed. "What ring?"

"Weren't you listening?" He cocked one eyebrow at her. "The one Sara and I bought you."

"You still have it?"

"In my wallet, in the back left pocket of my pants." He smiled at her. "Go ahead."

Sliding around on her knees, Aubrey lifted Jack's muddy, grass-stained tan corduroys off the backseat and pulled his wallet out of the pocket. She turned, sat, and opened it.

"Peel up the lining of the money flap," he said. "There's a key carrier underneath."

There weren't any keys, but there was a gold chain looped through one of the keyholes. Aubrey pulled it out and caught her breath as a wide gold wedding band plopped onto her palm. Her eyes teared and she had to blink furiously to find the catch and pry it open. Once the ring was free, she slipped it over the third finger of her left hand. It might, she thought, smiling as her eyes blurred again, fit better on her thumb.

"It's a-a little too big," she sniffled.

"Don't *cry,* Dumpling." Jack picked up her hand again and squeezed it tightly. "We can have it sized."

"That's not why I'm crying," she said as tears streamed down her face. "I-I'm just so happy."

They looked at each other, smiled, and then started to laugh. They kept laughing for twenty miles or so, until Jack's face was tear-streaked and they could both scarcely draw a deep breath.

"We've really had a wacky romance, my love," he sighed, still chuckling as he wiped the back of his left hand across his eyes. "Wouldn't you honest-to-God expect two adults to act like two adults?"

"Well, we did have a little help from our *friend,*" she answered pointedly.

Aubrey grinned at him, he grinned at her, and they broke out laughing again.

"Hey, aren't you hungry?" she asked.

"Ravenous." He leered at her. "But what I want I can't have and drive too."

"Would you settle for a Hershey bar with almonds?"

"If I have to."

Turning around again, Aubrey tugged the smaller of her grocery sacks between the seats and planted it between her knees on the floor of the front seat. She hummed happily under her breath as she fished out two Hershey bars and unwrapped one for Jack and one for herself.

"Oh, boy," she told him around a mouthful of almonds, "am I going to have to diet."

"You don't have to for me."

"I know that." She smiled at him. "I have to for me. I was miserable when I was fat."

"Are you sure it was your weight that made you miserable?" Jack crumpled the candy wrapper in his hand and tossed it at her.

"There you go again," Aubrey teased him. "Still picking on my poor mother."

"I'm not picking on your mother, Dumpling, I just asked you a question."

"I think you went into the wrong field, Dr. Draper. I believe you should have been a psychiatrist."

"In other words, mind my own business."

"No, it's just that I'm not sure which came first, the fat or the misery. They may have arrived simultaneously with puberty."

"Didn't your father die then, when you were about twelve?"

"Is the doctor in?" Aubrey asked sweetly.

"Okay, I got the message." He smiled at her. "Can I have another Hershey bar?"

"You bet." Aubrey grinned and dove into the sack again.

She felt so good that she had another one too. Then a Coke, and then another package of Sno-balls.

"This is terrific," she told Jack and wagged her eyebrows at him. "Guilt-free junk food."

"Enjoy, my love." He raised her hand to his mouth and kissed the back of her knuckles.

"What time will we hit the border?" Aubrey asked him.

"Sticking to the back roads will slow us up some," Jack answered, "but we should make it around three at the latest."

She looked at her Timex and saw that it wasn't quite noon. Three o'clock seemed an eternity away.

"We'll be there before you know it."

Famous last words, Aubrey thought, but smiled at him. Now that her stomach was full, the rest of her was beginning to feel cramped and achy from the long hours spent in the car, not only from this unscheduled trip, but from her long drive from Springfield to New York as well.

"I don't suppose," she said, thinking out loud, "that you'd care to change your views on luck in light of the fact that we haven't seen one police car since we left New York City?"

"No, I would not," Jack replied staunchly. "That hasn't a thing to do with luck. It has to do with the fact that we've stayed mainly on the back roads and well within the speed limit."

"Come again?" Aubrey asked dryly.

"Well, most of the time. Besides"—he glanced her a sideways smile—"I'm not exactly Public Enemy Number One, you know."

"Do you suppose the FBI will be watching the border?"

The second after she'd asked the question, Aubrey wished she hadn't, and looked sheepishly at Jack. He was frowning.

"I'm sorry," she apologized. "I wasn't trying to be the voice of doom."

"No, it's a valid question," he replied thoughtfully. "I honestly don't know, but I'll tell you this much." He paused and grinned at her. "If there is such a thing as luck, ours will probably run out there."

He was joking, but Aubrey wished he hadn't made the effort. A chill, not unlike the one she'd felt that morning when she'd been seized with that frantic need to be gone from the motel room, shivered up her spine. To take her mind off it, she retrieved her purse from the backseat, took out her brush, and tried to make something that at least halfway resembled a hairdo out of the frizzy auburn mop on her head.

Nothing worked but a rubber band and four bobby pins. She turned down the sun visor, rolled her head from one side to another, and made a face at her ponytail. It too was frizzy, but at least it was behind her where she didn't have to look at it.

"You wouldn't happen to have a tin of bear

grease in there, would you?" Jack asked, ruffling his left hand through his rumpled, spiky hair.

"No, 'fraid not," Aubrey laughed. "Heavens, you look like a startled squirrel."

He frowned at her, but his eyes were shining. "I *still* don't think that's funny."

Around one o'clock they stopped to fill the tank, and after two Cokes, Aubrey sighed happily at the sight of a clean ladies' room. Once they were back on the road, they ate again, fruit and cheese this time, followed by a box of Junior Mints apiece.

Right on schedule, at two forty-two according to Aubrey's Timex, the Camaro neared Niagara, New York. So far so good, she thought, and felt some of the tension she hadn't been aware of ease out of the muscles in her shoulders.

"Have you ever seen the Falls, Dumpling?"

"No, just pictures."

"Well, we can't have that," Jack said gruffly. "Every bride should see Niagara Falls."

"Does that mean," she asked hopefully, "that you're going to make an honest woman of me?"

"No, it does *not,*" he corrected himself adamantly. "It was just a figure of speech."

"Not a very funny one," Aubrey retorted and blinked back tears. "And that being the case, I really don't think we should fool around. I think we should just hie ourselves across the border PDQ."

"At this point in time, Dumpling," he answered her firmly, "ten minutes to look at the Falls can't possibly make any difference."

Ten minutes, she thought, might have made all the difference in the world this morning, and though she tried to argue Jack out of stopping to see the Falls, he would not be dissuaded. She gave it up finally and sat back in her seat, her arms folded, fuming silently. The back of her neck felt stiff and the beginnings of a headache throbbed in her temples.

Aubrey had always thought she was a whiz at hiding feelings, but Jack recognized the snit she was in the minute he parked the car. He shut off the engine and looked at her.

"Oh, come on, Dumpling," he purred, sliding his right arm around her shoulders and nuzzling her ear. "Humor me."

"I am," she snapped, flinging her door open. "Let's go see the damn thing."

As she swung out of the car she scooped up her purse from the floor and looped the straps over her shoulder. A not-so-faint roar filled her ears as she dug her sunglasses out of her bag and pushed her door shut with her left hip. Leaving Jack to lock up the car, Aubrey stuck her glasses over her nose and struck off up a slight incline toward a cloud of mist streaked with pale rainbows. She watched the pastel prisms, lavenders and blues mostly, gleam against the hot white sky, and thought again of the rainbow she'd seen around the lights in the lobby of Sara's building the night before last. Only two days past, yet it seemed like forever ago, and, remembering, she slowed down and waited for Jack.

Slipping his hand around her elbow, he smiled as he caught up with her. "I wish you'd cheer up," he said as they started up the hill again. "We're home free, Dumpling. The cops certainly have Collins in custody by now, Lawrence has the chip—everybody's happy."

Except me, Aubrey thought glumly, and wished she could figure out why. Though the two of them—she in her shorts and ponytail and Jack in his Cornell T-shirt—looked like any other couple of tourists come up to see the Falls, Aubrey couldn't shake her feeling of unease and kept glancing nervously around the crowd moving up the hill with them. Whom she expected to see she wasn't quite sure, but she kept looking anyway, while Jack rambled on in her ear about the volume of water that tumbled over Niagara every hour. His monologue bore a striking resemblance to the deadly barrage he'd harrangued Sara and her with on their canoe trip down the Current, and Aubrey was frankly glad for the roar of the Falls that drowned most of it out.

She hardly heard a word he said as he led her across a wide, concrete plaza dotted with striped patio umbrellas toward a high, iron railing enclosing the gorge. The scenery frankly didn't interest her, except when she recalled that she'd seen it all before in the movie *Superman II.* Because it was a memory that included Sara, it made her smile and momentarily suspend her scrutiny of the people milling around them. They'd seen the movie in Springfield, while Sara had been in town with a touring company, and her smile widened to a grin as she remembered how Sara had shocked her mother by wondering out loud in the theater if Christopher Reeve had worn a codpiece under his Superman costume. Leave it to Sara, she thought, to wonder about a thing like that.

Feeling Jack's hand slipping off her elbow as she went left and he went right, Aubrey corrected her course with a quick pivot on her heel. As she turned, a tall, wide-girthed man in a green Hawaiian print shirt, tan linen shorts, and a floppy-brimmed, plaid golf hat chose that moment to step between them. His shoulder caught hers, knocked her purse off her arm, and sent Aubrey stumbling backward. Although he was big, he wasn't at all clumsy, and with an open-mouthed look of dismay on his silver-bearded face, he wheeled around and caught her elbows in his hands.

"I beg your pardon, miss," he said, easing her gently back onto her feet. "Are you all right?"

"Oh, yes, I'm fine," she assured him, glancing from the partially spilled contents of her purse on the ground to Jack, who stood facing the rail about five feet behind the big man's shoulder.

"Here, let me," he said and knelt to help her collect her spilled purse.

"Thank you, but I can manage," Aubrey told him as she dropped to the ground beside him.

"Oh, no bother," he replied gallantly. "It's the least I can do."

"Really, I can manage," Aubrey insisted as she picked up her wallet in her right hand and reached for her bag with her left.

Her hand and his closed on the burgundy leather portfolio at the same time. She tugged at it, but his grip was like a vise, and a bubble of panic swelled in her chest as her gaze flew from her purse to his bearded face and narrowed blue eyes.

"Thank you very much, sir." She yanked again at her bag with both hands now as she let her wallet tumble to the ground. "But you've done enough."

"Oh, but, miss," he objected, and with a mighty

tug on her purse all but pulled her off her feet as she tried to rise.

Over the top of his plaid golf cap, she glanced up at Jack, who was just turning away from the rail with a quizzical look on his face. Their eyes met, his lowered, then widened as he pushed himself off the rail and leaped toward her. As she dug her heels into the ground to brace herself and pull, a flash of green winking in the sunlight caught her attention. About half a foot behind the man trying to wrench her purse out of her hands lay the Sheaffer Lifetime that Sara had given her.

Something stirred in the back of her mind—something O'Malley had said about Sara—as she stared at the fountain pen lying there gleaming in the sun. Her arms went lax and she released her grip on her purse. Still on his haunches in front of her, the big man in the Hawaiian shirt tumbled backward when she let go. He managed to fling out his right arm to break his fall, and as his palm struck the pavement it sent the Sheaffer rolling.

As it skittered toward the rail and the precipice beyond the something in Aubrey's brain clicked. Pearls. The green pearlized finish on the pen. With a wide-eyed shriek she dove after the Sheaffer as the big man rolled on his hip and caught her ankle. Falling forward, she kicked out of his grasp and felt the side of her foot strike something that was soft and hard at the same time. She heard him grunt behind her as she collided with the hot pavement, elbows first. The breath slammed out of her lungs and a burning, tearing pain shot up her arms—but the fountain pen was still wobbling toward the edge, and she lunged at it, scraping her chin on the tarry, sun-scorched macadam as she flung out her right arm and slapped her hand over the Sheaffer.

Sucking air madly through her open mouth, Aubrey sagged for just an instant, then closed her fingers around the pen, pressing the heels of her hands against the ground to push herself up. Her whole body throbbed and she could feel something wet trickling down her forearms, but she shoved herself to her feet and turned to face Jack with a triumphant grin on her face. It froze on her lips as did her heart between her ribs when she saw that he now stood flanked by the big man in the Hawaiian shirt and the two goons, Mr. Dark and Mr. Light.

If it hadn't been for the rail behind her, Aubrey thought later, she probably would have fainted and toppled over into the river, but as her knees buckled and threatened to collapse, the sun-warmed top iron bar pressed against the small of her back and pushed her up. Beneath Sara's blouse her skin burned and itched, but she ignored it as she looked around wildly for help, and realized there wasn't any. Certainly there were people close at hand, lots of them, all minding their own business and admiring the view. If any of them had observed her struggle with Hugh Lawrence–she'd figured out who he was a half-second after she realized she'd been carrying the chip around in the Sheaffer for the last two days–none of them gave any indication of it now.

For a wild second or two, as Lawrence gave Jack a shove to nudge him toward her and he and Mr. Dark and Mr. Light followed, she considered screaming for help at the top of her lungs. Almost instantly, however, she dismissed the thought when she realized that they most certainly had guns somewhere on their persons and that she could get someone—perhaps one of the children clinging to adult hands—shot or killed. So instead she bit her lower lip between her teeth, clutched the Sheaffer in her right hand for dear life, and backed away from them along the rail.

Neither Lawrence nor his two men made a move toward her. She wondered why, until she hazarded a glance at her right arm and saw how precariously close to the rail she was holding the pen. Quickly she looked back at Lawrence and saw him standing beside Jack, his bulk pressing him uncomfortably close to the railing. Behind them stood Mr. Dark and Mr. Light, the expressions on the faces impassive, almost bored.

"How very wise of you not to scream, Miss Nichols." His voice was low, but loud enough to carry the five or so feet separating them and override the dull thunder of the Falls. Lawrence smiled at her as he spoke. "I now propose an exchange—Jack for the pen."

"Don't do it," Jack began, then winced, and Aubrey bit her lip harder as she saw Mr. Dark move a step closer behind him. She took two more backward.

"Please, Jack." Lawrence laid an almost fatherly hand on his shoulder. "These are delicate negotiations." He looked back at Aubrey and smiled wider. "I, of course, further guarantee your safety. Give me the pen, Miss Nichols, and you and Jack may leave unharmed and with my thanks."

Pressing her left hand to her throat to still her frantically trip-hammering heart, Aubrey stared pleadingly at Jack. Almost imperceptibly he shook his head *no.* She nodded ever so slightly, then drew a deep breath and thrust her right arm over the rail.

Above his trimmed silver beard Lawrence's face went chalky. On Jack's left side Mr. Light moved; but with a sharp turn of his head and a quietly spoken word that Aubrey couldn't hear, Lawrence stopped him.

"Let him go first," Aubrey said, her voice quavering and her arm trembling. "Let him go and walk over to me or I'll drop the pen in the river."

While Lawrence considered, she avoided meeting Jack's wide-eyed, what-the-hell-are-you-doing stare. She hadn't the faintest idea what she was doing beyond playing the only trump card she had. Her aching, still-throbbing arm was getting very heavy hanging over the rail, and she wished Lawrence would unpurse his lips and say something.

"Your terms are unacceptable, Miss Nichols," he said and frowned. "The exchange will be made simultaneously."

"No, it won't," she answered as she let her tired arm droop lower. "It'll be made my way or not at all."

"Don't test my patience, young woman," he warned, his voice cold and harsh. "I've not come all this way to leave empty-handed. You now have precisely ten seconds to give me the pen or see Jack pushed over the railing—and don't think I won't do it. Crowds or not, I've already done one murder, and I won't hesitate to do another to get that chip."

She realized with a sharp intake of breath that

he meant Sara, and her gaze flew to Jack's tense, drawn face. *Don't do it,* his eyes pleaded, but she couldn't think of anything else to do. Fighting back miserable, defeated tears, she looked back at Lawrence and slowly drew her arm back over the rail.

"Very sensible, Miss Nichols." He smiled, took Jack's left arm in his right hand, and started toward her.

The two men had taken no more than three steps when Jack wrenched away from Lawrence, bent his left elbow, and rammed it into the big man's rib cage. As Lawrence doubled, Mr. Dark and Mr. Light sprang forward, and Jack whirled toward her.

"*Run,* Dumpling—!" he shouted at her, then spun back to face the two charging men.

Though her heart shot up her throat and a horrified little gasp escaped her lips, Aubrey had always done what she was told. Wheeling on her right foot and sucking a deep breath into her lungs she ran, ducking and dodging through the crowds.

# Chapter Thirteen

ONLY once did she look back, in time to see Jack throw himself at the ground and knock Mr. Dark and Mr. Light's legs out from under them. In that same brief glimpse over her shoulder, Aubrey also saw Lawrence, grim-faced, straighten and start after her.

Hoping that he couldn't run quite as fast as he moved otherwise, she turned to look where she was going and tightened her grip on the Sheaffer. She wished first that phys. ed. hadn't been her worst subject in high school, and second that she hadn't been thinking about those damn Hostess Sno-balls she'd bought when O'Malley had told her that Sara was mumbling something about pearls.

After that, she tried not to think of anything but breathing through her nose (that much, at least, she remembered from gym class) and putting one foot in front of the other as fast as she could. Her skinned knees throbbed with every stride she took, but Aubrey gritted her teeth, ignored the pain, and darted her way around the people strolling the paved promenade.

If she had any advantage at all over Lawrence,

she decided, it was quickness. Although he moved with remarkable speed and agility, in terms of body mass she had the edge. With that fixed firmly in her mind, Aubrey steered clear of open stretches of pavement where his greater strength, endurance, and longer legs gave *him* an edge. Keeping to the crowds, she ducked and wove a zigzag path and hoped to God she could lose him.

In her peripheral vision, Aubrey saw brief flashes of hey-watch-it-lady frowns cast in her direction as she bolted through the crowds. Once or twice, over the roar of the Falls and the thud of her own heartbeat in her ears, she heard a sharp cry or a shouted obscenity that told her Lawrence was pushing and shoving his way behind her. Although the thought of what his big hands could do to her if he caught up frightened her half to death, it also made her run faster, despite the wickedly hot sun beating down on her bare head and the tremor starting in her rapidly tiring legs.

The first time she stumbled and nearly tripped over nothing, it struck Aubrey like a fist in the stomach that she wouldn't be able to keep up this cat-and-mouse chase forever. Eventually, her legs and her wind would give out, and then Lawrence would easily be able to overtake her. A cold, nauseating wave of horror rippled up her spine, and she stopped, panting and trembling, to look over her shoulder and catch her breath. About fifteen feet behind her she saw him through a gap that opened suddenly in the crowd. He saw her too, unfortunately, and for a moment they just stared at each other.

In those few brief seconds, Aubrey noted his nearly scarlet face, heaving chest, and sweat-darkened hair clinging to his temples beneath his ridiculous golf hat, and recognized another advantage that she hadn't realized before. She wasn't sure of his age but knew that Mr. and Mrs. Draper were nearing sixty. If Lawrence was a contemporary of theirs, she reasoned, then with any luck, the heat would get him before he got her.

Hoping she was right, Aubrey wheeled and took off like a shot, glancing back over her shoulder to make sure Lawrence was following. She needn't have worried—he was, arms bent at his sides and his cheeks puffing. Good, she thought as she broke away from the crowds and ran straight for open ground. Tightening her grasp on the Sheaffer, she concentrated on keeping her weight on the balls of her feet and keeping her pace steady. Behind her she could hear his labored breathing, and she lengthened her strides, veering to the left, then back to the right.

She kept one ear trained on his heavy footfalls, hoping, *praying* for a break in their cadence that would indicate he was beginning to slow up. She never heard it, not even so much as a misplaced step, and the bubble of panic started swelling in Aubrey's chest again. The ground swam and spun up toward her as a wave of dizziness washed over her.

Don't quit, keep running, she told herself, then felt the graze of grasping fingers on her shoulders. Wrenching left to evade the hand that was groping at her, Aubrey heard herself sob as her knees buckled, and she lurched forward in a stumbling, running fall. She never hit the ground, however, but wished she had, as rock-hard fingers clamped around her right upper arm and jerked her around.

Every vertebra in her spine seemed to snap, and black spots swam in front of her eyes. A tearing pain lanced through her shoulder, and she blinked, scarcely breathing, as Lawrence's hand, fingers spread, closed on the pen clenched in her right fist. She wanted to scream but didn't have the breath for it, but she knew she had to do *something.* Like a vise, his hand clamped over hers, and, squealing in pain as she heard something pop and grind, she reacted out of instinct and bit him, as hard as she could, on the wrist.

He didn't cry out, he roared, and loosed his left hand from her arm to backhand her. She ducked the blow, felt a hot whoosh of air rush past her, and went down on her knees with her right wrist still trapped in his hand. His mouth was closed but he was still roaring, and the scorching wind of his breath was still tearing at her with cyclonic ferocity. His fingers were clawing at hers and she wanted to claw back, kick or something, but her field of vision was turning black and the roar of his voice was deafening.

"THIS IS THE FBI, LAWRENCE. YOU ARE UNDER ARREST. STAND BACK. THIS IS THE FBI—"

Wishful thinking, Aubrey thought dimly as she felt her body crumple in slow motion toward the ground. She heard rather than felt a sickening thud on the back of her head as the roaring voice slowly dwindled away inside her head.

She didn't wake up slowly but with a start that jerked her whole body convulsively. The ground wasn't hot and hard beneath her as she expected it to be, but soft. It smelled like stale onions. She heard somebody groaning and realized, with another start that jerked her eyes open, that it was *she.* There was a face above her, a blurred but familiar-looking face, and she shivered as a calloused, beefy hand gently patted her bare right forearm.

"Welcome back, Miss Nichols. How do you feel?"

The voice too sounded familiar, but Aubrey couldn't place it right away. She dragged the back of her left hand over her eyes, felt something stiff on her elbow as she did, then blinked up into Felix O'Malley's face. He still looked more like William Frawley than Efrem Zimbalist Jr., and she realized she was lying on the backseat of a car with her head in his lap.

"Am I—under arrest?" she asked haltingly.

"For what?" He smiled down at her.

Better let that one slide, Aubrey decided, and wiped her hand over her eyes again. A second, much more important question occurred to her, and she asked it in a small, shaky voice.

"Where's Jack?"

"In the ambulance over there."

*"What?"* She lurched up, but her head spun and she fell back on O'Malley's lap. "H-how bad—?"

"Just a crack on the head and some nasty scrapes." He patted her arm again. "Not as bad as yours, but nasty."

She raised her right arm this time and looked at the gauze pad on her stiff elbow and her first two fingers, splinted and taped.

"How did I do this to my hand?"

"You didn't. Lawrence broke two fingers trying to get the pen away from you."

"Why doesn't it hurt?"

"The paramedics gave you a shot the first time you came around, but I don't suppose you remember that, do you?"

"No, I don't. How's Sara?"

"Awake when I left the hospital and feeling pretty good, all things considered." His smile faded and he frowned at her as she lowered her arm to her side and looked up at him. "You were damn lucky, young lady. *Damn* lucky."

"I know." She smiled at him weakly. "Tell that to Jack, would you? He says there's no such thing as luck."

"I think he's been convinced to the contrary." His smile returned. "He and I had a very interesting conversation while the medics were cleaning you up. Lucky you stayed out for that."

"Yes, I'm grateful for that." She blinked back tears in her eyes and felt her mouth quavering. "I'm also grateful that you arrived when you did."

"So am I. Another thirty seconds or so and I believe Lawrence would've broken your hand and made off with the microchip. That would've been a real shame, 'cause the grand jury'll need it to indict Collins."

"You know about all that?"

"Of course I know all about it," he replied with a miffed little frown. "I've known all about it since I left San Diego two days ago. That's what I wanted to talk to Dr. Draper about in the first place."

"Oh, no," Aubrey groaned, and half-closed her eyes as she pressed the back of her left hand to the bridge of her nose. "I thought you wanted to arrest him. So did he."

"Yes, well." O'Malley cleared his throat. "We discussed *that* too."

"I suppose," Aubrey ventured in a sheepish voice, "that we really fouled things up, didn't we?"

"Yes and no." O'Malley shrugged. "Yes, you damn near got Sara and yourselves killed, but on the other hand, you nabbed Collins for me, and I've been trying to do that for months."

"Oh, well." She smiled tentatively. "I'm glad we didn't mess up *everything.*"

"No," O'Malley chuckled and patted her arm again, "just damn near everything."

"Do you suppose I could sit up?"

"If you feel like it."

With his hands pressed gently under her shoulder blades, O'Malley helped her. Though her head spun on the way up, once she'd turned around and leaned against the back of the seat, the dizziness passed.

"I suppose I'll be sore as a boil tomorrow," she told O'Malley.

"Yes, I imagine you will." He smiled at her.

"You're a very nice man, Mr. O'Malley." The corners of her mouth quivered again and her voice warbled. "I'm very sorry I caused you so much trouble."

"Well, that's all right." He mumbled a little and shrugged as he shifted his gaze away from her. "No real harm done."

"Thank you," Aubrey told him softly, laying her splinted fingers on his arm. "Thank you very, *very* much, Mr. O'Malley."

"That's okay, Miss Nichols." He covered her hand awkwardly with his. "You're welcome."

The back doors of a red and white ambulance parked twenty or so feet from the car where she sat with O'Malley sprang open then, and Jack climbed out. In addition to the white strip of gauze wrapped around his left arm, there was another circling his forehead. His face looked a little pale, but then Aubrey imagined that hers did too.

"Yo, Dr. Draper!" O'Malley called to him as he swung out of the car. "Over here!"

Pivoting on one heel, Jack glanced toward the car, and a wide grin split his face. He tried to run, but his left hand went quickly to his head, and he winced as he slowed to a fast walk. Watching him, the tears lurking behind Aubrey's eyes spilled past her lashes and she held her arms out to him as he stepped past O'Malley and slid into the car next to her.

"My love, my love," he murmured, embracing her and cradling her head against his shoulder.

For a long time he just held her, then he kissed her gently, leaned her away from him, and smiled.

"You look a lot better than you did the last time I saw you." He cupped his hands around her face and smoothed back the hair that had escaped her ponytail. "How do you feel?"

"A little rocky, but otherwise fine. How are you?"

" 'Bout the same with a splitting headache. One of Hugh's charming associates bashed me over the head with the butt of his gun. I cheered, let me tell you, when the local cops hauled them away."

"I wish I'd been awake to see that," Aubrey sighed wistfully.

"Don't worry," Jack chuckled. "You can watch the instant replay on the eleven o'clock news."

"Oh, God," Aubrey groaned. "My *mother.*"

"I think you'd better call her."

"I think you're right."

" 'Scuse me." O'Malley stuck his head inside the car. "You two are free to go—not too far, however. I'll want you to sign statements sometime tomorrow. Since neither one of you is in any kind of shape to drive, can I give you a lift anywhere?"

"Where to, Dumpling?" Jack asked her.

"I'd like—" Her voice cracked and she drew a deep breath. "I'd like to see Sara."

"So would I." He squeezed her shoulders and glanced at O'Malley. "Can you help us out, Mr. O'Malley?"

"As a matter of fact," he chuckled as he swung the door shut, "I just happen to be going that way."

Cuddling into the curve of Jack's arm, Aubrey leaned the back of her head on his shoulder. His body felt very warm and reassuring against hers, and her eyes drifted half-shut as O'Malley got in behind the wheel of the unmarked police car and started the engine. She sighed as the car rolled forward, then suddenly sprang up on her tailbone, her eyes wide open, as a helicopter, its rotors turning slowly, squatted like a giant insect on the pavement.

"Did you get here in *that?"* she asked O'Malley.

"Unfortunately," he grumbled over his shoulder. "I *hate* those damn things."

"Oh, good," she sighed, leaning back against Jack. "I thought I was hallucinating."

His arms enfolded her, and her eyes drifted shut

again. Because of the shot, she supposed later, she fell asleep almost instantly and slept all the way back to Ithaca. For the first time in years she didn't dream about Jack. But then, she thought, smiling as he wakened her with a kiss, she didn't have to dream anymore. She had the real thing.

It was nearly dark when O'Malley stopped the car before the front entrance of the hospital. The driveway looked familiar to Aubrey, but that was all.

"Are you sure this is the right place?" she asked O'Malley.

"I'm positive," he assured her as he kicked his door open.

"This doesn't look at *all* like the same place," she told Jack.

"You only saw the emergency entrance," he reminded her, smiling as he opened the back door, "and it was raining last night, remember?"

Last night. She rolled the words slowly in her mind as Jack got out of the car and offered her his hand. She remembered the rain all right, and so much more, and tried not to cry again as Jack gently helped her out of the car and onto the sidewalk.

"Hang on to me," she said giddily as her knees trembled. "My legs feel like Jell-O."

"Never fear, Dumpling." He wrapped his left arm around her waist, gently drew her right around his and held it there. "I intend to hang on to you for a very long time."

Their walk across the lobby and the ride up in the elevator with O'Malley seemed to take forever. When the doors opened on the second floor, Aubrey's knees threatened to buckle again and

Jack tightened his arm around her. She blinked a little in the bright white lights illuminating the nurse's station, and took a deep breath to still her rapidly beating heart as O'Malley pushed open the door to room 204.

Lying on her side watching the wall-mounted television, Sara glanced at them over her shoulder as they entered. Her eyelids jumped up a second before she did, and Jack handed Aubrey to O'Malley. Before Sara could throw back the sheet and leap out of her bed, Jack had scooped her up in his arms. Sobbing happily, Sara balanced on her knees, hugging him and thumping him on the back, then disentangled herself from his embrace and waved impatiently at O'Malley.

"C'mon, Felix," she chided him. "Get a move on it, will you?"

"Aw, keep your gown on," O'Malley complained beside Aubrey as he quickened their pace across the room, "we're coming."

"Oh, Sara, *please* don't hug me," Aubrey begged as Jack helped O'Malley ease her down on the bed beside Sara. "I hurt all over—"

"Oh, shut up, Nichols." Sara grinned and threw her arms around her.

Though it hurt like *hell*, Aubrey grimaced and did her best to hug Sara back. She also tried her dead-level best not to cry, but her eyes were streaming tears and she was hiccupping on sobs by the time Sara released her.

"Oh, Nichols, you blubbering boob." Sara laughed shakily, and her nose was red and her cheeks wet. "For God's sake, Jack, give me some Kleenex."

Smiling, he lifted a box off her overbed table

and handed them to her. Plucking out a handful, Sara blew her own nose, and Aubrey laughed.

"Here, Dumpling." Jack snatched several sheets out of the box and gave them to her as he sat down behind her on the bed, wrapping his arms around her.

"Well, folks." O'Malley yawned widely. "I'm bushed. See you in the morning."

"Hey, Felix!" Sara stopped dabbing at her nose as he walked toward the door.

"Yeah?" He turned back and frowned at her.

"Thank you." Sara blew him a kiss. "And don't forget to call your wife tonight."

"You're welcome." He chuckled. "And I won't forget to call Bernice."

"Good boy. Thanks again." She blew him another kiss, and the swinging door squeaked shut behind him.

"You two certainly are chummy," Jack observed dryly as he jostled Aubrey affectionately against him.

"I make friends fast." Sara winked at him, then smiled at Aubrey as she sat back on her heels. "And fast friends."

"When are you going to get out of here?" Jack asked her.

"Tomorrow," Sara answered, cocking her head to one side as she studied Aubrey's face. "Just in time too. Felix wired Mother and Dad this morning and they're flying home tomorrow night."

"Good," Jack said as he tightened his arms around Aubrey and leaned the side of his jaw against her temple. "You'll all be there for the wedding."

"Wedding?" Sara echoed, the little diamonds in

her eyes beginning to shine again. "Who's getting married?"

"Aubrey and I," he said, then added wryly, "finally, and no thanks to you."

An indignant frown puckered Sara's mouth, and Jack laughed as he leaned away from Aubrey and looked down at her.

"You will marry me, won't you?" he asked softly.

"I thought you'd never ask," she murmured around the lump swelling in her throat.

"We'd better clean up Mother's kitchen before we start making wedding plans," Sara put in. "If she sees that mess—"

"Who's this *we?*" Jack asked pointedly.

"Well, Aubrey and I, of cour—" Sara stopped short, blinked at her brother, then smirked and shrugged. "Okay, okay, I'll butt out."

"Thank you. And how do you know about the mess?"

"Why, Jack," Sara returned with a wryly arched eyebrow, "would Hugh have torn the place apart after he knew where the chip was? He was there when I got there, tried to give me some song-and-dance about how he found the place that way, which of course *I* didn't believe—"

"Oh, of course not," Jack chuckled.

"Well, I *didn't,*" Sara maintained staunchly. "And if all you want to do is play big, overbearing brother who saved my life—hah!—then you can leave and go get a cup of coffee or something. And bring me back a Coke while you're at it, will you?"

"I see." Jack chuckled in Aubrey's ear as he lightly kissed her cheek. "Want anything, Dumpling?"

"No." She smiled up at him as he rose off the bed. "Just you to hurry back."

"I will." He winked at her and squeezed her left hand. "You'll have to work fast, Heartburn," he told Sara over his shoulder. "I'll be back in ten minutes. I know that doesn't give you much time to grill Aubrey—"

"*Go,* will you!" Sara thundered at him, then made a face at Aubrey as the door swung shut behind him. " 'Just you to hurry back'? Oh, gag, Bree, try to remember that I'm sick."

"You look sick."

"I *am*—"

"Good." Aubrey smiled. "You deserve to be."

"I beg your pardon!" Sara jammed her hands on her hips. "After I risked my *life* to save that big jerky brother of mine who you love, God *knows* why—"

"He told me, Sara," Aubrey overrode her firmly. "He told me *everything.*"

"Well, high damn time, after he left me holding that damn chip—"

"No, Sara," Aubrey interrupted quietly. "He told me about Easter vacation and the ring and his phony fiancée."

"Oh." It was more an *ooh* than an *oh,* and Sara grinned sheepishly. "I meant well, Bree."

"I know that, and it's the only reason you're still alive."

"Well, what did you expect me to do? You two weren't getting anyplace, at least not with each other—"

"If you'd just left us alone—"

"You'd *still* be hemming and hawing around—"

"Draper!" Aubrey bellowed.

"Nichols!" Sara shouted back.

Red-faced and glaring, they stared at each other across a foot or so of white sheet. A commercial for McDonald's Big Mac drifted over the television screen: "Two all-beef patties, special sauce, lettuce, cheese . . ." Aubrey smiled.

"Forgive me?" Sara smiled winsomely.

"I suppose," Aubrey replied grudgingly.

"Well, don't do me any favors," she retorted sharply, but grinned.

"You'll be my maid of honor, won't you?"

"I'd better be."

"No hats," Aubrey told her firmly. "I look awful in hats."

"Okay, okay," Sara promised. "No hats. But no baby's breath either, not in my flowers. It looks like half-finished Q-tips."

"No baby's breath," Aubrey swore with a smile and sighed, "Oh, Sara, I'm so happy."

"You have me to thank for it, you know," she replied smugly.

"It kills me to admit it," Aubrey told her, "but I do."

"Good, that means you owe me one." Sara hunched forward eagerly. "And you can pay off right now, quick, before Jack comes back."

"How's that?" Aubrey asked warily as she turned her head to one side.

"Very simple, just answer one question."

"What question?"

"Is he any good in bed?"

"I heard that."

Laughing, Aubrey turned and watched Jack step through the door.

"You sneak!" Sara threw her pillow at him. "You never even left."

"That's right, I didn't." He walked back to the bed and sat down next to Aubrey. "Go ahead, Dumpling, tell her."

"Oh, never mind," Sara grumbled, folding her arms over her waist. "I don't want to know now."

"Maybe you don't, but I do." Jack slipped his arms around her and smiled. "So am I?"

"What do *you* think?" Aubrey asked softly as she parted her lips and kissed him.